Edendale

Edendale

Jacquelyn Stolos

Creature Publishing
Brooklyn, NY

Copyright © 2020 by Jacquelyn Stolos
All rights reserved.

ISBN 978-1-951971-01-4
LCCN 2020935433

Cover design by Keenan
Spine illustration by Rachel Kelli

CREATUREHORROR.COM
🐦 @creaturelit
📷 @creaturepublishing

For Andrew

Edendale

September

1.

Egypt knelt before her mirrored closet doors, imagining Lyle dead. There were so many possibilities on a weekday: the ceiling could cave in at his office or a crazed stranger could thrust a knife into his stomach as he walked to lunch. He could've died on the drive in, too, his brakes failing and his car crashing full speed into the concrete footing of an overpass. Egypt's phone would ring: the hospital. No, a police officer would knock on their front door with the news. Of course, the cop wouldn't need to say a thing because she'd know as soon as she heard his boots on the porch stairs. Women in love always know when they hear the boots on the porch stairs.

When none of this brought the necessary tears to her eyes, Egypt tried heart failure. Megan was always telling her these stories about seemingly healthy people who died in their sleep from defects they never knew they had, some kind of hole in some kind of chamber or a poorly developed tube that finally collapsed. This could happen to Lyle. She'd wake to his alarm and when she sleepily nudged him, annoyed he'd let it blare for so long, the weight of his cold stiff body would sit her up straight. She'd grab his wrist for his pulse and lower her mouth to his in desperate search for his breath.

Now, Egypt began to cry. She lingered in the imaginary moment. She'd grab him by his shoulders, sobbing things like *please* and *no*, or maybe she'd just wail in agony.

"Don't open that door," she mouthed into the mirror, because, of course, Megan would be at their door immediately.

Egypt, what's wrong? Egypt, let me in. Egypt, let me help.

Egypt took off her shirt to see what she looked like mourning in her little green bra. A thick line of clear snot shone from her nose down to her chin. She'd done it. Sniffling, she wandered across the hall into Megan's room. She stood just inside the doorway, watching Megan's gauzy curtains stir in the hot breeze. Megan's room felt brighter than the rest of the house. Her purple quilt was tucked into her mattress and, beside a vase of lilacs on her desk, three sharpened pencils of identical length waited in a neat row. She had framed prints, a color scheme, and her windows were the only ones in the house with curtains. Downstairs, the roommates had pinned a set of sheets to the front windows, flat sheet to the left and fitted sheet to the right. Sometimes, Megan would tie a knot in the bottom of each to let in some light. Egypt envied her for thinking like that. She envied her ability to have lilacs, to make her bed every day. Egypt had not been auditioning lately. Instead, she'd been spending her lonely weekdays wandering the shaded rooms of the house, staving off headaches with spoonfuls of strawberry jam. She'd come awake only in the early evening, when the threat of her roommates' returns finally propelled her into the shower.

It was early September, wind-heated and dry. They'd lived in the house on Lemoyne for just over a year: Megan in the front bedroom upstairs, Egypt and Lyle in the back, and Ropey down below, in the den off the kitchen. The den hadn't come with a door, so Ropey had nailed a tapestry to the wooden frame.

Three fires burned in a distant ring around the city. Reporters described neighborhoods evacuated, flames jumping freeways, and one family of five out in Palmdale who, too late to flee, survived a night in their swimming pool as their subdivision burned around them.

"We wet our tee shirts and draped them over our heads," said the father to a reporter, "keeping our bodies submerged to protect against embers. The water kept getting warmer. My wife told me afterwards she'd been sure we'd boil to death without knowing it. Like that thing people say about frogs."

When the roommates had moved in one year before, the house on Lemoyne Street had quivered with potential. With two whole stories, room for a kitchen table, and a backyard all to themselves, it seemed impossible that the universe could be so good to them. But time had passed. A yellow stain had bloomed across the kitchen ceiling. The sole bathroom was sandwiched between the two upstairs bedrooms and only accessed through each. The roommates sometimes found tiny lichen in the flattened carpet near the toilet. The back-right burner of the stove would never light.

2.

There were two memories of Egypt and Lyle to which Megan often returned. The first: Megan lay alone in the dorm room she'd shared with Egypt their junior year of college. It was a Tuesday. She'd just finished her reading, switched off her desk lamp, and climbed into her bottom bunk when she heard Egypt and Lyle coming down the hall. The door clicked open. Megan shut her eyes against the light cast onto her bed.

"Asleep," she heard Egypt say to Lyle. Their backpacks thudded onto carpet. Megan pulled her comforter over her ears to block the unzipping of zippers and the swish of discarded clothes. The couple climbed into Egypt's top bunk and Megan, used to willing herself to sleep beneath Lyle's heavy breath and Egypt's spoiled little moans, braced herself. But the slop of kissing did not come. Instead, the couple whispered to each other. Megan couldn't make out anything more than the rise and fall of their words.

She relaxed. Egypt and Lyle's voices blended together and their murmuring seemed to fill the room. Lulled, Megan drifted and warmed. The three of them were baby birds huddled beneath their mother's wing; they were the rocking timbers of a harbor-safe ship.

After nearly an hour, the whispering stopped. The room buzzed with silence.

"Guys?" she asked, forgetting she'd been feigning sleep, their unauthorized third.

"Goodnight, Meg," responded Lyle from above. "Love you."

The next: Megan sat with Egypt on a row of connected chairs in the baggage claim at LAX, waiting for Lyle. Megan and Egypt had graduated and moved to Los Angeles together one long year before, leaving Lyle back east to finish his degree. Now, he was joining them. His plane sat on the tarmac, waiting an eternity for an open gate. Egypt fidgeted in her chair so Megan offered her a snack. Egypt refused, saying she needed to walk around, and returned ten minutes later with a silver balloon that said *Welcome Home* in letters shaped from images of more balloons. A text update from Lyle: still no gate. Egypt gave the balloon to a girl sitting on her father's shoulders. She paced, wetting her lips with her tongue and smoothing her hair. When Lyle finally came through the heavy doors marked *Arrivals*,

Egypt ran over and threw her arms around his neck. The couple kissed to some scattered applause in the terminal. Lyle said hello to Megan, kissed Egypt again, and then excused himself to find a restroom. As he disappeared beyond a gray, rounded corner, Egypt began to cry.

"What?" asked Megan.

"He looks—"

Megan waited.

"I don't know," said Egypt. "He looks like how he looks. That's his face. But it doesn't feel like Lyle to me. Does that make any sense?"

"Not really."

"It's like this person is a perfect copy of Lyle. Everything's in place. Except something."

"What something?"

Egypt rubbed her eyes. "You know how when you look at someone you know, you recognize them?"

"This is Lyle. You don't recognize him?"

"No," said Egypt. "I do. I know it's Lyle. I just don't feel it."

Lyle returned from the bathroom. Megan watched Egypt closely. Egypt clung to Lyle's elbow while they waited for his luggage, smiling and stretching up onto her toes to kiss him at frequent intervals. It seemed to Megan that she recognized him enough.

Megan did not have a reservoir of memories of Ropey. For her, Ropey was just there, a coworker of Egypt's who happened to live with the three of them, lowering the rent. He was cool; she'd never met anyone who was just a bartender before. He turned their group of three into a group of four, a much better number, and he came with Captain America, the sweetest cat. Two men and two women: the order was sublime. Megan liked even numbers, clean surfaces, and tightly made beds. She often visualized the four of them as the points of a perfect square. In her square, their arrangement was constant: Lyle sat top left with Egypt below him, while Megan held the top right corner above Ropey. Some connections were stronger than others. The side between Egypt and Lyle was dense and compact, and a strong current ran diagonal between her and Egypt's points, pulling the two corners inward. So long as she didn't try to render her square physically, these contradictions didn't cause any problems. Her square corrected itself. It remained perfect.

3.

"We could wire the balance to your new account," the woman in the navy blazer told Ropey. Her name, Natalie, was engraved into the shining silver rectangle pinned to her lapel.

"Nope, just cash," said Ropey. Beneath Natalie's desk, he took his feet out of his sandals and rooted all ten toes on the bank floor.

In the main room, the weekday daytime people—the elderly, the young moms or dads, the hipsters—waited in line for the teller. This is where Ropey had been a few moments before, until the teller had panicked at his request and called over Natalie, who'd escorted him to this more serious corner of the bank. Apparently, a person may not take all their money at once, no matter how little they have, without causing alarm. Ropey shifted his weight, moving from pinky toe to big toe in an arc. He'd been working on embodying his whole body lately. He was skin, hair, blood, and he wasn't opening any new account.

The banker at the next desk wore a medical mask. That would be Megan soon. Ropey was fascinated by the effect that the heat and distant fires had on his eastern roommates. Each September morning that failed to deliver the relief of autumn wound them tighter. Today, when Megan and Lyle had collided in the kitchen, spilling coffee grounds across the linoleum, Megan's eyes had filled with tears and Lyle had punched an open cabinet door.

"Just the cash?" repeated Natalie.

"Just the cash."

A lifelong Californian, Ropey knew wildfire season: the ash, the longing, the psychic itch of thirsty skin. He also knew that relief wouldn't come until the wind switched directions and carried the first winter rain in from over the Pacific.

"Full name here," said Natalie, "and sign here." The hair on her upper lip caught the light and glowed in a way that made him fall in love with her a little bit. Ropey signed his full name, which always felt to him like someone else's shoes, and Natalie brought him his balance in a slim white envelope. *Get yours, too, and let's run away*, he thought. He and Natalie could drive down to Mexico and use her blazer as a picnic blanket on the beach. They'd have a son with dimples and a daughter with a limp.

Edendale

"Anything else I can help you with today?" Natalie asked.

"I think we're all good." Ropey smiled.

Officially unbanked, Ropey bowed goodbye to his banker wife and dipped back into the world. Outside, the city was wonderful, terrible, a mess of stucco and chain link all drying up under the wide, low sky. Ropey's favorite thing about Los Angeles: without a natural harbor or freshwater source, there's no topographic reason for LA to be. Instead, there's the diverted Colorado trickling in on cement and the feeling that everything could crack up or burn down. He'd once heard a stupid rumor that LA existed simply because of the flattering afternoon light. As Ropey left the bank just after four, everyone did look beautiful. The old lady selling empanadas, the stylish couple in heavy boots. What else was beautiful was the way that it felt to have all his money in his pocket, the way the bad sky looked through the leaves of the broad ficus tree.

4.

From seven to seven, Monday through Friday, Lyle sat at a marble counter in a long white corridor answering an important Hollywood phone. Lines flashed, his inbox filled. Throughout the day, Lyle took care to drink only enough water—he could never be sure when his next chance to pee would come.

Up and down the corridor, other assistants sat at matching marble counters answering matching phones. They were people with big ambitions, all making slightly above minimum wage but dressing like executives and meeting for cocktails on hotel rooftops after work. All except Lyle, who wore a suit his father had purchased in the nineties and drove the long commute home after work to drink cheap beers in his cheap yard. He cultivated this image, setting out his brown bag lunch where everyone could see. Before meeting Egypt, he'd had no specific career ambitions, just an interest in economics and a desire to make an above average amount of money. Now, he was going to be a Hollywood agent.

At 2:43 and a half, Lyle took off his headset to fetch the agent her Diet Coke. He knocked on her door at exactly 2:45 p.m. Lyle took pride in being good at his job.

She was mid-thought when he entered her office.

"The valet has my keys," she said without looking up. "Just go down and take it from my trunk and put it right in yours. I know you're here all day but you've got Egypt and all those roommates at home and I'm freaking out, everyone in this city is going to get cancer." She drank the Diet Coke through a straw to preserve her teeth.

"Thank you," said Lyle. He noted that, on rich women, age looked more like a stiffening than the shriveling and drooping of his mother and aunts. "Your six o'clock pushed to next week."

"I have those drinks, tonight, though?"

"Seven thirty."

"Why don't you go down to the garage, now, then." she said. "I can't drive around with that thing any longer."

Lyle rode the shining elevator down to the garage. While the valet was retrieving the agent's car, Lyle sent Egypt a text. *Hello! I love you! You're beautiful!*

It was an air purifier, brand new. He lugged it to his Civic as the valet returned the agent's car to the part of the garage where the nice cars went, wondering if he'd someday be the kind of boss who found pleasure in giving extravagant gifts to his assistants. Receiving was slightly demeaning, but it was also nice to have nice stuff. On the ride back up, Lyle imagined himself returning home with the air purifier this evening and setting it up in their living room. They'd all dance and clap and swoon with gratefulness. Trumpets would trumpet. *Oh Lyle, you hero, you man!*

5.

Egypt knew she should be grateful. That he was good and she was bad, even worse for resenting him for taking care of her so well. She thought this as she lay in the bed he'd bought for them to share. It was evening. Above her, dark thick dust accumulated in the tracks of the sliding window and on the plastic panels of the vertical blinds.

Now, she heard him on the stairs. She should be grateful but instead she was angry. His competence spotlighted her incompetence. His kindness sharpened her meanness. She despised how she was in reaction to him.

And then here he was, lugging some new machine into their room. His suit was rumpled and very uncool, but he preferred it that way.

"Air purifier," he said. "From Wendy. She's thoughtful, concerned about you here all day breathing this shit in."

"I'm not here all day," said Egypt. "I have a job." She didn't really have a job. She was scheduled to host a couple times a week at Little Wink and was the first called off when things were slow.

"Right," said Lyle, lying down beside her. "Sorry."

"I'm getting ready to do more auditioning."

"I know you are."

"Things have been hard."

"You don't have to tell me."

"I want to be the kind of person that things are easy for."

"I like the kind of person you are."

Since she could remember, Egypt had been operating under a theory in which true love stripped away a person's inessential layers, showing lover to lover completely, illuminating the dark corners of each of their essential selves. What was love if not complete knowledge, a total merging?

Lyle stood to plug in the air purifier. She knew and didn't know him. She loved and didn't love him. The air purifier whirred on, a little light at the top glowing red.

"Oh!" said Lyle. "That means the air is full of particles!"

She could have told him that. Her eyes watered and her nose ran with each wildfire breeze. As he tinkered with this new machine she hadn't asked for, anger rose in her chest.

"Come here," Egypt said, and he did, so she tamped down the anger and doubt by straddling him on the bed and unzipping the fly of his pants.

"You're so pretty," Lyle said.

"I am," said Egypt. She took off her shirt. He reached up immediately to latch his pink hands onto her breasts. She imagined how she, a topless woman straddling a rumple-suited man, would look to someone observing from the door. She instinctively arched her back. Lyle fumbled with her nipples, his expression simple and happy. Egypt exhaled grandly for the doorway observer.

"You like that," Lyle said. The observer turned into Ropey and Egypt rolled onto her back. She again formed a picture of the two of them. Lyle, dog-like, licking at her rib cage. Her, pale and indifferent.

"I like that," she said.

6.

Aware that too much space made children anxious and wild, Megan kept her classroom partitioned by a network of waist-high cubbies. With the help of her two classroom aides, she spent her days rotating her students through this network in small, strategic groups. Today, it had been rainforest puppets in the Story Center, engineering blocks in the Math and Science Center, and a Rubbermaid of turquoise sand in Imaginative Play. Megan knew her students needed structure and routine. They needed controlled environments to explore and little nooks where they could hide. Megan also knew that she was the same kind of animal as her students. She was careful to divide her own days into small, digestible pieces. Wake up, run, work, spend time with roommates, read and reflect, then sleep. She knew that if she thought of life as anything more than the accumulation of these pieces, she too would be made anxious and wild by its vastness.

Edendale

The turquoise sand had been a mistake. The color had rubbed off—why hadn't she predicted that food dye would rub off?—and so the last half hour of the school day had been a mad rush to clean the evidence of her mistake off two dozen sets of little fingers before parents and nannies arrived. Now, it was very late and she'd reached the end of her Lysol wipes and her classroom was still spotted with turquoise fingerprints. Megan took out her planner and noted *sand-colored sand* for next year. She turned off the lights and sunk down into her chair, listening to another lingering colleague walk down the bright hall. Megan loved the sound of footsteps echoing down a school hall. Sometimes, she wondered if she'd chosen her profession because of it. Yes, she believed in children, in education, and the goodness of the two, but she didn't feel as though she needed them. What she needed was the echo of a practical shoe on school linoleum; she needed stacks of colored paper, bins of safety scissors, and the smell of pencil shavings as she emptied them into the wastebasket at the end of the week.

At home, Megan showered right as she came in. She read for thirty minutes and journaled for fifteen before turning out her light.

* * *

"Meg?"

Megan woke as Egypt—her bare arms and legs cool, reptilian—slid into her bed. "Hey Meggers, can I sleep in here with you?"

Megan opened her eyes to the pre-dawn gray of her room. Here it came again. "What happened?"

"Nothing happened."

Megan sat up and flicked on the bedside light. "No, not nothing."

"Please let it be nothing right now."

"Are you hurt?"

"No."

"Sick?"

"No."

On the other side of the bathroom door, Lyle coughed. Together, Megan and Egypt stiffened, drawing in their breath. They listened as he flushed and ran the faucet. The floor creaked as he walked back into the room he shared with Egypt, closing their door behind him. Megan let go of her breath.

"Okay," she said, turning off the light and sliding down beside Egypt. "But we need to talk about this." They'd lived together for six years, in nine different homes counting their college dorms. There'd been

Edendale

bunk beds, futons, and an air mattress on the floor of a sublet in Van Nuys, where Megan had spent a week combing lice eggs from Egypt's scalp each morning. Another time, after Egypt backed up into a pot of boiling water, Megan had cleaned and dressed the burn. Megan began to rub the familiar topography of Egypt's back. After years of zipping her into dresses and popping unreachable pimples, Egypt's body seemed a nerveless extension of her own.

Megan slipped out of bed a few minutes after dawn. She tied her running shoes and stretched her calves on the front porch. On Lemoyne, she passed a cluster of tents in the sandy median, admiring the tarps strung above and the neat broom lines in the dirt. As a child, Megan's favorite fantasies were adventures turned domestic. She imagined herself a person who could build a home on a desert island from wreckage, making a neat bed from the twisted wing of the aircraft and a set of bowls from coconut shells. Thinking of coconuts, thinking of Lyle—he'd wake soon, had he even slept?—Megan turned onto Baxter, which she liked because it ran straight over the hill instead of snaking around it. She focused on her breath and the ground directly in front of her. She ran up to an oil spot, to the shadow of an overhead branch, to a crack in the sun-bleached asphalt, not seeing the coyote until she was nearly upon it.

Megan stopped short. The coyote stood in the center of the street, head low, spine and shoulders jutting, its patchy fur matted with seeds and thorns. Around its eyes, red sores oozed like mouths. Megan's pulse beat against her skull. She held her arms out wide, knowing that a person is supposed to make herself large when encountering a predator, and backed slowly down the hill. The coyote didn't snarl. It didn't follow her. It simply watched, the smoke breeze ruffling its raised fur.

Back on Lemoyne, Megan spotted Lyle walking to his car. As she slowed to speak to him about the night before, his expression warned her not to mention Egypt.

"Coyote up on Baxter," Megan said instead. "We need to make sure everyone's keeping the cat inside."

He shook his head, eyes grateful for her omission. "They're moving in on us," he said.

7.

Egypt woke alone. She showered and dressed purposefully, untangling her wet hair with fast strokes of Megan's brush. Finished, she strapped on her best sandals, hurried down the stairs, and broke into the heat of the day before the concavity could reemerge, trapping her at home again.

Resolved to spend her day happy, productive, away, Egypt picked her way down Lemoyne Street to Sunset. She walked to the park where she stood beneath a palm tree watching joggers stretch, mothers push strollers, and tourists steer paddle boats around the fountain at the center of the manmade pond. Here was the world. Here were people, living. Children whizzed by on scooters and Egypt noted the speed with which they kicked the cement away. She noted the triangles of sweat soaking the joggers' backs, the light blankets draped over the mouths of the strollers, and the moss drying in the cement folds of the Lady of the Lake's nine-foot skirt. Egypt stepped from the shade onto the footpath, resolving to stay out until after Lyle arrived home from work. She imagined how she'd look to him, blustering in flushed with the day's private experiences. For a moment, she felt attractive and large.

After three laps around the lake, her dress was damp beneath her armpits and the crotch of her underwear was close and sticking. Sweat mixed with the sidewalk grime on her feet, causing her to slide forward and strain the straps of her sandals. Her resolve began to flicker—even her best sandals were on the verge of breaking—so she rushed over to a water fountain, gathered her hair at the nape of her neck, and bent to drink. She tried to steady herself. She'd lost her knack for it all: for keeping herself clean, for maintaining a respectable fleet of clothes and shoes, for strolling through a park on a summer day. Yet, she was here. That had to count for something. An airplane buzzed overhead. Egypt looked up to find it in the yellow sky, and, as she turned back to the cool arc of water, something light but hard and sharp hit the center of her back. She reached between her shoulder blades and discovered liquid, warm and sticky. Beads of it rolled down her spine. Looking down, she noticed a crushed Pepsi can in the grass. She turned. Ten yards away, a woman in a set of shimmering pajamas cowered

Edendale

by an overturned recycling bin. The woman's feet were bare amid the spilled plastic and glass. Worry surged up Egypt's chest—this woman would cut her feet.

"Ma'am," said Egypt, starting toward her. The woman reached down, picked up a glass bottle, and hurled it at Egypt. The bottle hit Egypt square in the throat. Egypt coughed, stepping backward. This woman was throwing trash at her. Egypt stepped forward again, asking the woman if she was all right. The woman lowered her pants to the ground, stepped out of them, and began pulling at the buttons on her shirt. Unable to grasp her buttons, she pulled the top over her head and threw it down into the pile of trash. She was naked. Egypt stared. The woman had a sculpted stomach, an even tan, and the wormy nipples of a mother. Her arms were slim and her skin smooth with upkeep. The woman hunched forward, trying to cover herself with her hands. Her eyes darted left and right. Egypt followed her gaze. The park had stopped around them. Mothers stood protectively in front of strollers, and joggers, paused and sweating, gaped. Suddenly, Egypt hated the woman for singling her out.

"Your pajamas are right there." Egypt pointed. "You took them off yourself."

The woman raised her face to Egypt's. Lipstick stained the creases of her mouth.

"Right there. Look."

The woman did not look. Instead, she ran at Egypt and pulled her into a hug. She grabbed Egypt's skirt, wrapped it behind herself for cover, and held tight. Sky and park stirred around them. Though the world remained—there was the sound of sirens; there was the smell of wildfire carried into the city by the hot breeze—it all seemed thin and unreal compared to the pressure of the woman's embrace. Egypt felt herself shrinking, condensing, soon she'd transform into a pit or a seed and clatter down onto the sidewalk between this woman's bare feet, until two sets of large hands appeared and pulled the woman off and away.

After two male police officers wrapped the woman in a blanket and helped her into an ambulance, a female officer stood with Egypt in the shade of a gnarled sycamore and recorded her statement. Egypt was surprised by how easy it was to communicate the mechanics of the story: the woman had thrown trash at her, taken off her clothes, and then wrapped herself in the skirt of her favorite yellow sundress. Though she relayed this information exactly as it happened, Egypt couldn't shake the feeling that she was lying. She looked everywhere but at the officer. Nearby, a vendor with a gleaming metal cart shaved ice for children in white

Edendale

and navy uniforms. The pajamas remained on the grass beside the trashcan.

A breeze made the fine hair on Egypt's torso stand. She looked down, noticing that her dress was torn at the seam. It swelled open with each gust of wind, exposing her from rib cage to hip. When Egypt gathered the material in her fist to close it, the police officer chuckled.

"Sweetie," she said, "if I had a waist like yours, I'd make sure everyone could see it."

The officer offered Egypt a ride home, but she insisted on walking so she could call Lyle. Lyle's phone went straight to voicemail. The strap of her sandal broke halfway up the hill toward home. She carried the shoe the rest of the way, stepping lightly on the hot asphalt with her one naked foot.

The house on Lemoyne was blue with dirty white trim. Nestled into the base of the Edendale hills where the city grid dissolved into snaking canyon roads, the house was oppressive, dark, and rotting. There was a porch, a dried-up front yard, and two low peaks on the roof. A slope of golden brush rose up behind it. Egypt paused outside the gate. She didn't want to go back in, but it was hot on the street so she pushed open the gate and walked up the front path. At the door, she discovered she'd forgotten her key. She looked back out toward the road. The porch faced southwest. On a clearer day, a sliver of ocean would have been visible on the horizon, but today, the sky was thick with wildfire smoke blown down from Ventura. Egypt sat, pulled her knees to her chest, and waited for someone to come home and let her in.

8.

Megan stopped for groceries on her way home from work. In the supermarket, she tossed the tortillas, the tilapia, and the cilantro into her basket with a happy flick of her wrist. All day, she'd had a dreamy picture in her head of the four of them sitting at the picnic table out back around plates scraped clean, filling and refilling their wine glasses. She'd plug in the string of white lights and bring some candles out to the table. She'd have dinner ready before either of the boys arrived. When Megan got home, Egypt was on the front porch hugging her knees. Megan shouted something about dinner—I'm making fish tacos, get hungry—and Egypt looked up with a face that made her set her groceries down by the gate and hurry up the walk. She sat down and wrapped Egypt in a hug, rocking her back and forth until she began to breathe audibly, then, finally, cry.

"What?" Megan asked. The bag fell over. A lime rolled into the street, its downhill progress stopped by a wide crack in the pavement. "What what what?"

The dress had once been Megan's. Egypt looked gaunt, prepubescent in it, as she did in all of Megan's discarded clothing.

Megan helped Egypt inside. She helped her wash her face and her feet as Egypt called Lyle again and again.

9.

On the night of the afternoon when the woman in the park had ripped Egypt's yellow dress, after the sky had darkened, after Megan had plugged in the string of lights and lit candles on the picnic table, after they'd cooked and eaten tacos and rinsed the plates clean, Ropey was holding Egypt's smallest toe, painting its pebble of a nail when Lyle walked out onto the patio. Though her cold foot remained in his grasp, Ropey felt her slide away. The yard tilted. All the comforting that he and Megan had done was instantly undone.

"You didn't come," Egypt had said to Lyle.

"My phone. I didn't know," Lyle said. "Babe, I'm so sorry."

10.

"Come on. You've got to get out of the house," Ropey said the next day. "It's our morning off.'"

Egypt had a lot of mornings off. She told Ropey so.

"That woman ripped my dress yesterday," she said.

"Wear another?" suggested Ropey.

She wanted to be a woman for whom it was that simple, so she faked it, following him down the hill to a coffee shop, where Ropey, wary of air-conditioning, insisted on the patio. Too much time in artificial temperatures could sever one's connection to the natural universe, he explained, and if a body forgot it was of the earth, well.

"Well, what?" Egypt had asked.

"You've got to know where you're from."

Egypt didn't like to read. She flipped the pages of *Judy Garland on Judy Garland: Interviews and Encounters*—hardcover, a gift from Lyle, who'd stayed out very late last night, when she'd needed him most—then, bored, peered into the dense row of hedges that separated the patio from the street. A few cigarette butts, the snapped half of a credit card. Something speckled and twitching gave her a quick start, then she realized it was only a leaf. She turned back to Ropey, whose forehead folded into fat wrinkles as he squinted at his book. As she considered the folds—he'd have permanent lines there soon—his lips began to move. His eyes, still on his book, brightened like they did when he was flirting.

"What?"

Ropey looked up, startled. "What?"

"You're smiling."

Ropey reddened and turned back to his book.

"What are you smiling about?"

"Nothing, really."

"C'mon." Ropey was a pushover. She liked this about him.

"I don't want to embarrass him."

"Embarrass who?"

"Lyle."

His name always made a little something in her leap. Egypt thought of Lyle at his desk with his headset and swivel chair, Lyle not knowing that she was out with Ropey.

"What about Lyle?" she asked.

"It's his book."

Ropey turned the book around to reveal a page heavily annotated by Lyle's blue pen. Egypt reached for the book, but Ropey pulled it to his chest. "Something about this seems private."

"But you're reading it. I'm his girlfriend."

"Right."

"Exactly."

"Exactly. That's why I'm not going to let you read it."

"Is there something about me in there?"

"No."

"Then what?"

"Who would you rather confide in, a stranger or your closest friend?" asked Ropey.

"You're not a stranger to Lyle."

"You know what I'm saying."

"I do," said Egypt. "But I don't think you're right. I think if Lyle was here, he'd show me."

"You're probably right," said Ropey. He closed the book. "What does Judy Garland have to say about Judy Garland?"

"Lyle's notes."

"Egypt."

"The way you're acting is making me think there's something nasty about me in there," Egypt said. "You're not making me feel good at all."

Edendale

"You know that Lyle couldn't even think anything nasty about you," said Ropey.

A flicker of warmth beneath Egypt's cheeks. She desperately wanted and didn't want to be seen straight through.

Ropey took a long sip of his coffee. Ice cubes emerged yellow as teeth. His nails were short and clean, which surprised her. She became very conscious of his breath. She moved her foot so that the rubber of her sneaker pressed against the rubber of his and watched the contact register in his eyes.

"We should go," he said, standing. "I have to shower before work."

At home, she lay on the floor beside her closet, looking at herself in the mirrored doors as she listened to the hiss of his shower. Her legs were very white, her knees dry. She considered going into Megan's room to search for some lotion; she considered water, how the water from Ropey's shower would dry out her skin further, and how she took that knowledge for granted, but that, once, discovering that water dries a person's lips and skin instead of moistening them must have astonished her. The shower turned off and Ropey left the bathroom through Megan's room. Egypt remained on the floor, listening to his downstairs sounds, until she heard the front door slam behind him.

The book lay on the foot of Ropey's bed with his discarded shorts and towel. Egypt picked it up and opened it, hurrying through Lyle's notes. She found nothing that made her want to smile the way Ropey had, nothing intimate at all. She glanced over the notes once more. Just the typical Lyle things. *Person = good only if actions = good. No inherent self.* Captain America wandered out from under the bed.

"Do you see it?" Egypt asked the cat.

The cat crouched in defense, like she'd thrown something at it. Staying low to the ground, he darted out of the room.

That she knew Lyle was the most solid fact of Egypt's life. She was sure that, in finding him, she'd located herself. Still, there was some kind of fog. When had it come? Egypt was sure she'd once dug all the way to Lyle's core, but she couldn't remember the moment of finding, couldn't summon what it had felt like at all. She looked down at the page again. There were Lyle's notes. The familiar shape of his letters, his slight *o*'s and *a*'s, his tilting *t*'s and *l*'s.

Captain America crept back into the room. He rubbed against the foot of Ropey's dresser. Lately,

Edendale

Ropey had been depositing his tips into a shoebox in his top drawer instead of into his bank account. When no one was home, Egypt liked to take out the money to sort and count it, just to feel the volume of wrinkled bills in her hands.

Now Egypt divided the money into piles of fifty on Ropey's bed. Tending bar, Ropey got a single for every drink he poured. Hosting, Egypt got her waist pinched. She got winks and raised eyebrows. She counted the piles, mussed them up, and then sorted them again. Captain America watched from the windowsill.

"I'm just sorting," Egypt said. "He'll appreciate it." When a bird landed on the sill outside, distracting the cat for a moment, she pocketed a few twenties.

11.

In the quivering blue twilight, Lyle paused on the front walk listening to his roommates' voices float up from behind the house. Here was a happy screech, there, a snort, and, from the brush, pleasant nighttime chirps, croaks, and rustles. Still, his chest remained tight, his shoulders clenched. Like a child whose bed ebbs and rolls after a long day of playing in the waves, Lyle held the pace of his desk even when he was away from it. He had to remember who was on line six. He had to order dinner—poached chicken, no skin, brown rice—exactly forty-five minutes before the agent would want it. Whenever he began to drift, Lyle felt the urgent tug of an email unanswered or a studio head on hold.

The front door opened.

"Lyle?" called Egypt, peering out from behind it.

Lyle felt discovered, a fool. "Hi," he said.

"Hi. Thinking of coming in tonight?"

Edendale

Lyle followed Egypt inside and up the stairs. As they ascended, he studied her heels, cracked and white, and the fringe of dark hair growing above her right ankle. It was a small relief whenever he discovered a patch of her body he didn't want to put in his mouth, his desire for her normally so intense that life outside her crawled with discomfort. In their room, he set down his backpack and pried off his shoes. Egypt sat on the foot of the bed. She sucked her cheeks, her lips pursing. He knew that look. She was thinking, waiting.

"What's going on?" asked Lyle.

"I told myself I'd give you some time to unwind."

He watched her fists clench and unclench. Lyle placed his shoes in the closet and knelt on the carpet in front of her, taking her fists in his hands.

"What?" Lyle asked again.

"I hate ambushing you right when you get home."

Lyle waited.

"It's the bed again."

Lyle nodded. He'd thought they'd solved this one already. It seemed so simple to him: they'd needed a bed so he'd purchased one. But Egypt didn't like simple. She liked to tangle things up and then writhe around in the mess. She liked to be inconsolable. And this worked for him. He liked to console.

Lyle released Egypt's hands and moved down to her feet, rolling each clammy toe between his fingers and thumb. He wanted desperately to take off his suit. He only owned the one and felt he'd soon sweat through his shirt.

"What kind of woman doesn't have a bed?"

The word *woman* sounded ridiculous to him. Lyle thought of himself as *boy* and her as *girl*, picturing them as hairless twins curled together in a pink womb. "Not you," he said.

"A weak one."

"You have a bed. We have a bed."

"I have a place to sleep in exchange for sex. That's almost prostitution."

"We've got a bit more going on than sex, babe."

"If things changed between us, I wouldn't have a place to sleep."

Suddenly, the state of their bed seemed atrocious to him. Sheet flung one way, comforter dragging onto the floor. Lyle dropped Egypt's feet and made the bed around her. As he tugged, folded, and smoothed, he considered telling her that if she wanted some ownership over the bed, perhaps she could make it when she got up each afternoon. He lifted the mattress, tucked the sheet, and chose not to.

"I don't make the bed," Egypt said, "because I have never made my bed. It isn't necessary. It's an imaginary chore that you think needs to get done but actually doesn't."

Lyle set to work on the corners. He was proud of his ability to make a bed so correctly. He imagined Egypt complimenting his precision.

"If I made the bed," she continued, "it would just be another service I'm performing to earn my place in it each night."

Lyle said nothing, not wanting to reveal that the way she argued disgusted him. Immature, self-satisfied, and, like the hair on her ankle, a small relief.

"You don't need me."

"I do."

"Not financially."

When he didn't respond—sometimes he didn't have a response: she was small and lovely, he liked the smell of her mouth, it was only a bed—she complained again that he didn't need her. He put his head in her lap. I need to put my head in your lap, he wanted to say. I need you to let me buy the bed.

"What kind of woman," Egypt started again, then trailed off.

By now, the glow of twilight was nearly gone and their walls, his dresser, and hers had all faded to gray. Lyle looked into mirrored closet doors. There they were: a couple in bed. It was a good bed. He'd read so many reviews and spoken to half a dozen salespeople about the way her legs got restless, tingly, around four or five and she had to pace through the house for a while before she could get back to sleep. He'd found the right bed for her.

Egypt sniffled. He felt her expand and contract with each angered breath. With each trivial argument, she was digging toward some other, deeper source of her discontent. Selfish, he didn't want her to find it.

12.

Ropey, sitting cross-legged on the living room carpet, scooped up a handful of marbles and dropped them into the hollows of the mancala board. Finished, he nodded to Lyle across the coffee table. Lyle leaned forward, careful not to wake Egypt who was pretending to doze with her head on his lap. Ropey watched as Lyle counted out each potential move.

"Clock's ticking, man," said Ropey.

Egypt moaned in her sleep. This irritated Ropey. He knew she was awake, knew the moan was a performance intended for Lyle, enhanced by his presence. Once, in a conversation that Ropey later regretted for allowing to become too intimate, Egypt told him that she faked sleep whenever she needed a certain kind of attention from Lyle.

"He'll do things like lift up my shirt and stare at my boobs," she'd explained.

Egypt let out another moan and rolled over, nuzzling her face into Lyle's lap.

"Oh, you're awake," Ropey said to Egypt. He looked up at Lyle. "You know she's awake."

He wanted to put his hands around her waist. He knew that's what she was going for, and it annoyed him, but the awareness and the annoyance also made him want to do it more.

Lyle shrugged and made his move. He'd win. Though the two had learned to play together, Lyle normally won because he was a deliberate guy, a counter. Ropey admired this. If Ropey were ever tasked with rebuilding his personality from bits and pieces of others', he would take quite a few of Lyle's parts. Lyle was the type of person who noticed inconsistencies on their utility bills, calling the electric or water company whenever something didn't seem quite right and getting them a few bucks back. For his birthday last year, Lyle had drawn Captain America stretched and curled into each letter of "Happy Birthday, Dear Ropey," even the comma.

Captain America tiptoed into the room, sat down, and began to gnaw the dirt out from under his claws. Watching the cat, Ropey made his move.

"You want to take that back?" Lyle asked. Ropey looked down at the board. He'd set Lyle up for immediate victory.

Ropey opened his arms wide. "Demolish me," he said, and Lyle obeyed with a smile.

"May I play winner?" Megan called from the top of the stairs.

"Why don't you take my spot," said Lyle. He ruffled his hand through Egypt's hair. "I'm going to take this girl up to bed."

"She's awake." Ropey said. He reached across the coffee table and plugged a finger into each of her nostrils. "You're awake."

Egypt opened her eyes, swatting his hand away. "I am now," she said. "Asshole." From his vantage point on the floor, the violet skin beneath her eyes looked papery, ready to tear.

13.

Their sophomore year of college, Egypt became the darling of a group of film guys, all seniors. Each night, she fluttered around campus for rehearsals and shoots, meeting Lyle at the library café for midnight coffee breaks, flushed with activity and attention. It was all very sexy to him. He escorted her to the film festival in May ready to burst with pride. She starred in six out of the ten entries that year. In five of the short films, she was killed. Once by her father, once by her fiancé, and three times by a stalker. In the sixth, she was a mistress who killed her lover when he refused to leave his wife. Lyle had sat beside her in the theatre, captivated by all of these dead and murderous Egypts, playing with the knees of the real one, the one he'd take back to her dorm and fuck.

"To emote," she whispered, craning her mouth up to his ear in the dark theater, "I imagined everyone was you."

14.

There'd been a small incident during the shooting of one of these short films. Caught up in the excitement of a dorm room scene, Egypt had taken off some of her clothes and felt invigorated, nearly drunk, by the startled, hungry way the boys had looked at her. So she'd taken off more of her clothes. Lying on her back on the low pile carpet with her thumbs tucked into the elastic of her underwear, she'd felt invincible, the most interesting person in the world. She removed her underwear. None of them removed anything. They took turns twiddling and pawing at her. She felt at first like a sexual renegade, then a little unsure, then suddenly very distant, like it was a thing she was hearing about that had happened to someone else long ago, not a thing currently happening to herself.

Egypt didn't cry until three days later. The tears came unexpectedly during her urban anthropology class. She couldn't stop so she walked very quickly, head down, out of the classroom to the bathroom, where she stayed hidden in a stall, biting her hand to stifle her sobs, until the period was long over.

15.

"I'm adamant about my bartenders' shirts," Lisa, the weekday manager who desperately wanted weekends, called across the restaurant. Egypt rolled a fork, knife, and spoon into a napkin, trying to block out the whine of Lisa's voice by turning her mind toward images of Lyle: Lyle biting his tongue as he maneuvered into a tight parking spot, Lyle arguing the price of oranges with the carnicería, Lyle, last night, when she gave him sixty dollars toward her half of the bed and he'd held the money limp, away from his body, as though she'd handed him a dead fish. She hated Lisa. Part of it was her voice—the whine, the babyish inflection—and part of it was that she was always throwing her arm around Egypt, declaring them twins. Egypt saw no resemblance. Lisa needed to lose thirty pounds and her eyes were horrendously close together.

"You live with him, can't you do something about his shirts?" The whine was directed at Egypt then, but from the way Lisa stood curved toward the bar, Egypt understood the performance to be for Ropey, who was prepping the garnishes. Though Little Wink opened at eleven on weekday mornings, the restaurant rarely had a customer before one. These two hours were for cleaning and prep, plus puttering around trying to seem busy while flirting with each other. The guys in the kitchen rolled up towels and whipped the back of Egypt's knees whenever she went out back to retrieve clean glasses or silverware.

"I'm thinking of you," Lisa said, slinking up to the bar. "I'm thinking of your tips." She took an orange slice from Ropey's cutting board. She put it in her mouth.

Egypt set down a cluster of forks. They hit the table louder than she'd expected. Ropey and Lisa turned to her.

"Careful with those," said Lisa.

"Sorry," said Egypt. "I wouldn't want to break the forks."

Raising her eyebrows, Lisa turned back to Ropey and stole another orange slice off his board.

Later, while walking home in the early evening heat, Egypt tied a knot in her shirt at her waist.

"I've neglected to dress you. Think you can forgive me?"

"I might have it in me." Ropey picked a lime off a branch hanging over a fence.

"Maybe I can help Lisa out, too. Get her some pants that do a better job containing."

"Be nice."

"I'm being funny. I'm trying to make you laugh. She can criticize the way you dress, but I can't criticize the way she dresses?"

Ropey put the lime in his shirt pocket. "Just be nice."

"You're smiling," Egypt said. "How am I terrible if you're smiling?"

16.

The cat lay across Megan's desk as she journaled neatly about the panic rising in her chest. It was all just so messy, so out of control. She wanted to go out there and put the fires out herself. She scratched the cat between his ears and felt something rough on his skin. She spread his fur, examined closer. A scab, small and tight.

Captain America yawned, stretching his legs and fanning out his paws. Between two of his toes, Megan noticed a small, dry burr. She picked it out, held it up to her face. Had he been outside? He couldn't go outside.

17.

Ropey opened the front door to Egypt lounging on the sectional—one knee seductively bent, an arm flung behind her head, shirt up above her belly button—thumbing through Lana Turner's memoir. *Lana: The Lady, the Legend, the Truth*. She turned toward the door with a smile but sat up quickly, righting her shirt, when she saw it was him. This was the hour when Lyle usually arrived home.

"Sorry to disappoint," he said.

"What?"

"I'm not who you're posing for."

"I have no idea what you're saying."

Ropey imagined her arranging herself carefully on the couch, bending her knee just so before lifting her shirt to make it look like it rose by accident. He bet the book was a gift from Lyle. He bet Egypt had been the kind of kid who pretended to faint when her parents' attention was elsewhere.

"How's Ms. Turner? Has she killed her husband, yet?"

"Ex-lover. And it was her teenage daughter."

"Her daughter was her ex-lover?"

"No. Her daughter had the kitchen knife. I'm not posing."

"What are you doing?"

"I'm reading."

"Okay," Ropey said.

"I'm not posing for Lyle."

"You're not posing for Lyle," Ropey said as he walked through the kitchen into his room, where he found Captain America on the foot of his bed with a squirming finch in his mouth. The idea that Egypt had guessed he would arrive before Lyle popped into his mind before he squashed it. The bird was still alive.

"Give it," Ropey said, reaching toward the cat. Captain America looked Ropey straight in the eyes and bit down hard. There was a pop and a single, panicked squeak as the cat's tiny incisors pierced the finch's flesh. Its small, gray talons curled and then released. Captain America turned, walked up the bed to Ropey's pillow, and dropped the bird. Its wings fell open as it landed on its back, small, dark droplets fanning out on the sheet around it. The cat looked to Ropey, back at the bird, then back up at Ropey, his head tilted in expectation.

Edendale

"Jesus," said Ropey and the cat jumped down off the bed and ran into the kitchen. Ropey glanced around the room for something he could use to pick up the bird. He noticed his tee shirt drawer ajar, his money box on the floor. He opened it. Yes, there was a bit missing. Not enough to change his or the taker's finances, but enough to make a point. He looked again to the blood on the bed.

18.

"I need your opinion," Lyle said to Megan, who sat at the kitchen table with her bowl of yogurt, damp curls hanging close to her face. He took Egypt's torn yellow sundress from a plastic grocery bag and laid it across the kitchen table, spreading the seam open where it was torn. "I was thinking I'd get this fixed. A surprise."

Megan wiped her hands on her napkin and then ran her fingers along the seam.

"Oh, that's easy," she said.

"So you think it's a good idea?"

The idea was a week old, born when the dress fell off its hanger and slithered down to the floor as Lyle whipped through their closet, looking for a clean shirt. The dress was made of something slippery, not silk because there was no way Egypt would own real silk, but some kind of synthetic fabric manufactured to feel like silk. He picked it up. The way it slid around in his hands reminded him of the way it clung and slid as she moved, making her seem more naked underneath the dress than she was when she was actually naked. It drove him crazy. She knew it drove him crazy and used to wear it two, three times a week. He'd get it fixed—because he liked it, because she liked that he liked it, because the day when the woman in the park ripped it, he hadn't been there to protect her. Instead, for the first time, he'd turned off his phone and left work early to get drunk with coworkers on a patio under a tree hung with dozens of brass lanterns, failing her.

"It shouldn't cost too much. If I had my machine, I could do it for you for free."

"No, I mean, do you think Egypt will like it?"

"Like it?"

"The dress."

"Why wouldn't she like it?" Megan turned the dress inside out, inspecting the intact seams. "It's hers."

It was a comfort that Megan saw the world the way that he did. It was Egypt's dress. She would like it. He was a good boyfriend, and the kitchen was sunny and bright.

"I can't give you my opinion unless you tell me what you want my opinion on," said Megan. She set her spoon down into her bowl with an authoritative clatter and took the two to the sink.

"She's been upset about the bed, lately," said Lyle. Immediately, this felt like a betrayal. But he wasn't attracted to Megan. The effort she put into her horse-like face. After breakfast, she'd go upstairs and dry her hair with that big round brush, making herself look ridiculous.

"What's wrong with the bed?" Megan asked.

"I paid for it."

"She'd prefer if you'd stolen it?"

"No, she'd prefer if we'd split the cost."

Megan nodded. "I can see that."

Lyle grabbed the dress and stuffed it back into the plastic bag.

"This is how things go with couples," he said. "Someday I'll be sleeping in a better bed paid for mostly with money she's earned, but it'll be ours."

"Earned how?"

"Acting."

"Lyle."

Lyle's jaw clenched.

"Okay," Megan said. "Can we restart this conversation? I want to help with this dress project."

Lyle knew from her smile that she was genuine. Everything about Megan was straightforward, clean, and true.

"I don't even know where to start with seamstresses," said Lyle.

"Most dry cleaners do repairs."

"Oh. Thanks."

Edendale

"And I'll talk to Egypt about the bed."

"No, please don't."

"I think I should."

"I'd prefer if you didn't."

Later, while driving to work, Lyle thought of Megan's sewing machine. If it wasn't here, where was it? Still, he imagined her lifting it down from the top shelf of her closet and teaching him how to sew. He'd fix Egypt's dress, he'd sew pillows and curtains for their house, he'd buy reams of that cheap, embroidered silk from Chinatown and surprise each of his roommates with a colorful, patchwork robe. The four of them would billow around Edendale, shining like kings.

19.

"And then Megan made me toss my sheets," said Ropey. He dried the final wineglass and hung it on the rack. "Don't you think that's a bit extreme?"

Lisa put both hands on the bar, tossed her head back, and laughed. They were the last two at Little Wink and Lisa sat twirling on one of the stools, agreeing with everything he said. Tonight, Lisa loved cats. In fact, Lisa would love to meet his cat. Captain America sounded like a funny little punk, pulling that trick with the bird.

"She even bought me a new set," continued Ropey. "Made my bed up for me while I was here last night."

"That's amazing."

"She's amazing."

"She's a preschool teacher?"

"The very best."

"I should live with a preschool teacher."

"Everyone should live with a preschool teacher."

Lisa demanded another shot.

"You too," she said, pointing to Ropey's empty glass.

Ropey filled their shot glasses, which they cheersed together, whisky splashing onto their fingers.

"It seems you've gotten me drunk," said Ropey.

"Oopsies."

"That's quite an accomplishment."

"Hmm?"

"Getting a bartender drunk. It's an accomplishment."

"Why?"

"I'm always drinking. Never drunk."

"You're always drunk." Lisa slid off her stool, walked around to his side of the bar, and tilted her face up to his, presenting herself for a kiss.

"Now, manager," Ropey said. "You're drunk, and you're my manager."

"You're drunk and cute."

"That's a strong argument."

"What about me?"

"What about you?" Ropey grabbed her wonderfully fat butt. Flesh was a lovely thing.

"Am I cute?"

"Oh, so cute. Unbearably cute."

They moved quickly through some kissing and groping, then each took off their shoes, pants, and underwear. Naked from waist to socks, Lisa lay down on the thick rubber mat behind the bar.

"Room's spinning!" she announced.

Ropey knelt down onto the mat between her legs and eased himself into her. The mat, sticky with spilled drinks, made a ripping, Velcro sound each time he shifted her in a way that pulled her bare skin away from its surface.

"Sorry," he tried to say into her mouth, but she was sucking very hard. She came or pretended to come after only a few minutes. Ropey sat back onto his heels.

"You're good?" Lisa asked.

"Yeah."

"I'll be fine if you need to keep going."

"Nah, I'm hammered."

Lisa giggled.

Ropey stood and poured them each a glass of water. He drank his in three gulps as she dabbed herself clean with a bar rag.

"I think that's a dirty one," he said.

She bent over, stomach laughing, and tossed the rag over the bar into the dark restaurant. He found her a fresh one and watched as she continued to clean herself. The sight of her crouched over the bar mat in just a shirt, her waxed crotch chafed red and puffy, aroused a rush of sympathy in him that felt a bit like love. He walked back over to her, cupping her pubic bone and kissing her forehead.

Edendale

"Want to sleep at my place tonight?"

"Why?"

"I think it would be nice."

"Okay." Lisa raised her eyebrows, put on her pants and shoes, and followed him out.

Walking back to the house on Lemoyne, they came upon three coyotes in the street. Heads low, pendulum tails swinging. Ropey's breath caught in his chest, but Lisa pulled him forward. The coyotes dispersed, slinking between the street-parked cars.

Night was night, with its rushes and stirrings, its dome sky above and city grid below. With Lisa's elbow locked onto his, Ropey felt less of a longing to share it with someone than he usually did. On the porch, they stepped out of their shoes and kissed again. Her mouth, warm and wet, seemed enormous, like he was about to tumble in. When he opened the front door, the stale yellow interior light took him by surprise. He'd half-expected night to be everywhere. His three roommates, spread out over the sectional, all blinked at the open door.

Megan broke the stillness. She stood, extended her hand, and introduced herself. Lyle followed suit, offering Lisa the bong. Lisa accepted. Egypt remained silent. Her face was small and red.

"Ropey was telling me about the bird." Lisa spoke out a mouthful of smoke.

"We have quite a cat," said Lyle. "An accomplished hunter, a real sportsman."

"He had to get some new sheets," said Megan. "You wouldn't think there'd be so much blood in one little bird."

"There wasn't really that much blood," said Ropey.

"Well, it was more than I'd expect, anyways," said Megan.

"But not that much," offered Lyle. "And now he's got new sheets."

Megan and Lyle held their smiles for a moment too long.

"Hey, do you mind cleaning that off," Egypt said, gesturing toward the bong in Lisa's hands.

"Egypt," said Megan.

"Her mouth was on it," said Egypt.

Lisa wiped the mouth of the bong with the bottom of her shirt. She turned to Ropey. "Where's your room?"

"Through the kitchen."

Lisa set the bong down on the coffee table. "Goodnight, Egypt."

Ropey led her into the kitchen, smiling apologetically when his tapestry door came into view. Most women were too tactful to object to his living situation, and some seemed to consider his poverty romantic. He tried to lead Lisa to his bed, but she stayed in the doorway.

"Hold on." She held out the tapestry like a matador. "Hold on."

"Sorry," he said, but Lisa laughed. She dropped the tapestry and took off her shirt. She wore a purple bra with large, shining cups. He took off his own shirt and pressed against her. She placed her socked feet on his and they rocked back and forth in a sort of slow dance. From the living room, he heard Egypt ask Lyle if he was ready to go upstairs. Lisa led Ropey to the bed. She removed her pants, then his, then lifted the sheets and climbed in. Ropey followed. They faced one another on Ropey's single pillow. Her forehead shone with grease and her cheeks were flecked with dried mascara.

"Do you want to sleep naked?" she asked.

He removed the rest of his clothes as she removed hers. She slept with one soft arm and leg over his body. He felt he didn't sleep at all, but suddenly it was morning and she was gone. The other side of the bed was cool.

Ropey pulled on his jeans and stepped out into the bright kitchen where Lyle flicked a fork through a bowl of pancake batter. He wore swim trunks and a Hawaiian shirt. Egypt sat on the counter beside him, wearing a pair of Lyle's checkered boxers and a cotton bra.

"Morning, Ropes," she said as she ripped open a package of bacon with her teeth.

"Shit," said Lyle. "Didn't realize you were still sleeping." Egypt peeled a single slice of bacon from the clump of fatty meat. Lyle continued. "We're going up to Malibu today. You want to come? Does Lisa want to come?"

"She can borrow one of my suits," Egypt said. She dropped the slice of bacon onto the frying pan. As it popped, grease splattering up, Lyle pulled Egypt backwards. He covered the pan and then took off his shirt, draping it over Egypt's bare shoulders.

20.

Whenever the four of them went somewhere, Lyle drove. His Civic was old but reliable, and he was proud of his Kansas plates. Windows open, Ropey sat shotgun in charge of the music, while Megan, back right, navigated them through traffic using three separate apps. Egypt sat behind Lyle. Never buckled, sandals off, stretching forward every few minutes to scratch her fingers through his hair. Whenever she dragged her nails across the nape of his neck, Lyle felt he understood dogs.

The entire flat grid of Los Angeles, with its strip malls, its baked-in grime, and its startling pockets of white mansions on green lawns, lay between Edendale and the beach. On and off the freeway, through neighborhoods with rusted chain-link and neighborhoods with yellow speed bumps twice each pristine block, they stopped for coffee, stopped for snacks, stopped to pee in a grocery store parking lot because Egypt was sure she'd piss her shorts if she tried to make it inside. Hair whipping, clothes fluttering, they reached the coast and Lyle turned north toward where the mountains curled down beside the ocean, sleeping dinosaurs. Each curve in the highway gave way to views of cliff, sea, and fog, making Lyle wonder aloud about wildfire, but Ropey declared that the fog was just fog.

"You guys get so freaked about fires. They're normal. They're natural."

Lyle parked the Civic on the northbound shoulder to avoid paying for the lot and they sprinted across the highway when there was a break in traffic. Through the gravel parking lot, past a picnic table gray and prickly from salt, Lyle led the way with the red cooler, followed by Megan and Egypt each with sandals in hand. Ropey trailed, spinning the frisbee up into the air. The stairway down the bluff was part wood, part rock, and part hard-packed earth.

"Someone had to *make* these," Megan said. They were paused at the curve of the first switchback, ocean wind ruffling terrycloth and hair.

Admiration for whoever built them flickered through Lyle. The wind caught Ropey's frisbee mid-toss and lifted it back up over the bluffs.

"Shit," he said. "I'll meet you guys down there."

Edendale

The remaining three finished the trek down. On the beach, they paused for a few minutes to watch two women in evening gowns writhe around in the sand for a photographer looming above on a wooden box, then trekked past a rocky outcropping to an isolated cove. Megan and Egypt spread their towels while Lyle explored a sea cave tucked into the bluff.

"I bet this thing fills up at high tide," he shouted back to them before he disappeared.

"Let's live out here when we're rich," Egypt said, burrowing her toes into the sand.

Ropey made drinks for the girls—red wine mixed with Diet Coke in the can—then raced Lyle down to the water to toss the frisbee in the surf. Megan rubbed sunscreen into her darkening thighs—spraying a bit over Egypt's shoulders, too—as Lyle and Ropey drifted further from shore with each throw and catch. When they were out past the breaking waves, Lyle floated onto his back and froze his body in a perfect "T." As a teenager, he learned from a Red Cross tutorial that this was the best way to conserve energy when stranded in open water. Now, he practiced every time he swam. Ropey treaded water, holding the white disc above his head. Lyle closed his eyes against the bright sun. Yes, he could float like this for a very long time.

"I'm into her," Ropey was saying, "but I don't want to disturb my balance. I tend to find equilibrium solo. Plus we work together."

Lyle opened his eyes. "Sorry, what are we talking about?"

They slid down into a small valley before bobbing up another wave.

"Lisa," Ropey said.

The salt was beginning to burn Lyle's eyes. A wave buoyed them up.

"Oh. Right."

The frisbee caught the wind and escaped Ropey's grasp. The men watched it blow toward shore.

"Lisa," said Lyle. The rhythm of the waves was making him dizzy. A worry almost recognizable tugged in his chest. He wanted Ropey to date Lisa quite badly.

"Yeah. She's pretty chill."

"She seems it."

A wave broke behind them. Lyle let it carry him to shore.

Egypt woke to Lyle dripping over her, his head a black spot in the sun.

"Tide pools?" he asked.

She put on her sunglasses and held both hands forward so that he could pull her to her feet. He led

Edendale

her to the edge of the cove, where the bluffs bent into the ocean. They scrambled over the black, craggy rocks, letting go of each other's hands for balance. Egypt found a rock shaped like a chair and sat, watching Lyle step carefully over the sharp rocks that jettied out into the ocean.

He bent, poked at something that she couldn't see, then turned to her.

"Babe," he called. "Starfish."

Egypt walked out to meet him. The starfish was a fleshy peach, like the inside of another animal.

Egypt reached into the sun-warmed pool.

"Do you think we look alike?" she asked.

The starfish remained motionless beneath the rippling water as Egypt swam her fingers towards it.

"You have nicer legs, but she has more."

Egypt snorted. "No, me and Lisa."

"You and Lisa?"

"Me and Lisa."

"No? Yes? Honestly, I don't really remember what she looks like."

Egypt brushed the tip of the starfish with her index finger. The animal convulsed, spreading like a hand, then all five limbs curled into themselves.

* * *

The sun blazed. The roommates dozed. Egypt and Ropey shared a small dose of mushrooms. Everyone kept wandering away to dip in the ocean or climb up into a cave. They ran out of water. Gulls rode the cresting waves, and reptiles skittered over hot rocks.

"Hey!" A firefighter, in full gear, trudged toward them from around the rocky outcropping. "Hey!"

Megan hid the wine. Lyle walked up, responsible.

Egypt watched as they conversed with expressive hands. Lyle, pale in navy swim trunks. The firefighter in his thick boots, pants, and jacket. He held his helmet under his arm. She thought maybe he'd come wrap her in a blanket.

Lyle jogged back.

"We're advised to leave," he said.

They packed quickly. "They're just being careful," said Lyle. "It's not quite the evacuation zone, but it's windy today. Things can spread fast."

Back up on the highway, they used the beach blanket to wipe the fine layer of dust off the car windows.

"That's not ash, is it?" asked Megan.

"I think it must be," said Lyle.

Edendale

"This is kind of fun," said Egypt. Her heart beat quickly. Her face felt flushed. A helicopter padded overhead, disappearing behind the mountains. She imagined a wall of flames rising over the hillside, but the sky remained a dull, hazy blue.

21.

They had dinner and drinks at a thatch-roofed Thai place by the beach and drove home on the winding canyon roads, making it back after midnight. Edendale was full of cars idling with flashers on to drop passengers in front of bars. Smokers gathered on the sidewalks beneath eucalyptus trees. Every few blocks, someone grilled—ribs, quesadillas, hot dogs wrapped in bacon—on a grease-dulled cart. Lyle waited at the light to turn onto Lemoyne. Across the intersection, a man dragged a woman by the waist through the Rite Aid parking lot.

"Ropes, do you see that?"

The woman struggled against the man's arm.

"See what?"

As Lyle pointed, the woman landed a kick on the man's shin. He stumbled backward and she bolted, but, before she was out of reach, the man grabbed her wrist. Both fell to the asphalt. The man stood quickly, looked around, then pulled the woman back up by her armpits.

"Shit," said Ropey.

"What?" asked Megan from the backseat.

"Across the street."

The light turned green. Lyle drove across the intersection and into the lot. As he pulled up beside the couple, the man let go. The woman took off. She ran out of the lot toward the dark, residential streets that led up into the hills.

Alone, the man waved at them, smiling nervously, then crossed his arms over his chest. Lyle got out of the car. He heard Megan and Ropey do the same.

"Everything okay?" asked Lyle, tongue thick and stupid.

"Hi. I know how this looks. That was my girlfriend. I'm just trying to get her home safe."

"Oh."

"Yeah."

"This is awkward, but, it looked like maybe she was trying to get away from you?"

"She does that sometimes. When she's drunk."

"Oh, um, okay."

"I need to go find her, now."

Lyle looked towards Megan and then Ropey, who each stood inside their open doors. Neither's expression told him how to act. As always, he wanted to act correctly. He looked down the street where the woman had disappeared, then into the backseat. Egypt's white face floated in the dark.

The man hurried back toward his car. "Thanks so much," he said. He slammed his door and drove out of the lot, turning onto the street where the woman had run. In the empty lot, the Saturday night noises settled around them: bar voices streaming off open patios, sirens in the distance, the pop of firecrackers somewhere in the hills. Far away, a coyote yapped. Closer, another howled in response. Megan cleared her throat. Ropey sniffled.

"Do you think he was telling the truth?" asked Lyle. "About her being his girlfriend?"

"Would that change something?" asked Ropey.

"Well, if he was trying to take care of her."

"She didn't seem too eager to be taken care of." Ropey squinted, critical.

"I don't know. When you see a thing like that from so far away," Megan said. Then: "Remember when Egypt used to get drunk and bolt?"

A small animal—a stray cat, or maybe a raccoon—ran low across the far side of the lot.

"We never had to grab her like that," said Lyle.

"I did," said Megan. "All the time. Let's go home."

"I'd like to call the police," said Ropey.

"What are you going to tell them?" asked Megan.

Edendale

"What we saw."

"Do you remember the make or model of his car? The color? The license plates?"

"The car was dark green."

"Let's just go home," said Megan. "That was probably their foreplay or something. Pretty girls like to get chased."

Ropey huffed.

"Call the police if you're going to call the police," said Megan. "I'm not stopping you. I just don't really think it's necessary." The roommates waited. A helicopter, carrying water, passed, heading east.

"Okay," said Ropey. "Yeah, I guess you're probably right. We can go."

Lyle, hesitant, climbed back into the driver's seat. Conscious of Egypt, silent and tense behind him, he turned left out of the lot toward home. Beyond those hills: the valley, and beyond the valley: the smoking San Gabriels, which, in cooler seasons, were peaked with caps of white. Lyle didn't realize he half-expected the woman to be on their porch until he pulled up and felt relief to discover no one crouching there in the dark.

October

1.

During the first week of the hot month of October, a raw patch of flesh appeared and opened between Captain America's shoulder blades. The sores expanded rapidly. As the autumn heat settled into the house on Lemoyne Street, the cat bled on the sectional, across the kitchen linoleum, and in all three beds. Each time the sore began to crust over, Captain America dragged himself along a doorframe or some other hard corner, tearing the scab away and painting a long, red streak across the wall.

"The vet," said Megan to Ropey as she blotted a fresh streak. She couldn't believe she had to suggest it.

"You think so?" Ropey stood in the center of the kitchen, rubbing the cat's stomach with his long bare foot.

"Look at our walls."

"He'll scab over soon."

"I'm cleaning bloodstains off our walls."

"Just leave them. It's fine."

"Leave them?"

"We're renters."

Megan brought the sponge over to the sink and wrung it out beneath the tap, surveying her cuticles, now pink and swollen. She and Lyle had been scrubbing all week. They'd tried everything from industrial grade cleaners to homemade baking soda pastes, but red only gave way to brown, and brown only gave way to slightly lighter brown. When the sponge water ran clear, Megan turned to face Ropey.

"That veered off in the wrong direction," she said. "I'm concerned about the cat, not about the wall." On the floor, Captain America purred beneath Ropey's foot, eyes half-closed in pleasure. "When are you taking him to the vet?"

"You think it's that bad?" With his blue eyes brightening with worry, Megan could nearly understand how other women looked past his rancid beard, finding him attractive.

"I do. He looks thinner to me, too."

The kitchen window let in a smoky gust. Megan reached over the sink and slammed the pane down. The now constant smell of wildfire had awakened something deep in her guts. It spread outward with the slowness that accompanies sureness, a snake sliding patiently through her veins. Leave, leave. She fought it. At school, Megan had abandoned her Underwater Worlds unit, making up a new curriculum on the fly about the role of wildfire in the western forests' natural cycle. She hung a laminated diagram of seeds activated by heat, fertilized half this year's batch of bean plants with ash, and read a storybook about a family of field mice who burrowed deep into the mud to wait safely as the flames passed overhead. Each night, the news played images of tendrils of smoke rising from blackened neighborhoods, the loaded cars of evacuees backed up on canyon roads. There was one farm out past Big Bear where a cluster of charred equine remains inside a meadow gate told of the horses' trust in their farmer's return. The farmer, who'd been kept away by a police blockade on one access road and flames across another, wept openly each time he explained to reporters that his horses could surely have collapsed the fire-weakened gate in stampede. Megan brought a park ranger into class, who explained how, without wildfire, forest systems would grow too dense and choke themselves to death. As he spoke, Megan had circled her classroom, placing her hand on each restless shoulder to remind her students to sit criss-cross-applesauce. Be still, tiny darlings. We are safe here in the city.

* * *

"We're having a hard time," said Lyle, in bed, to the sharp bones of Egypt's back. "Couples go through hard times, but that doesn't mean it has to end." Lyle waited. Before work, he had to bathe, dress, strip their bed, and pack his lunch, but first he needed her to understand. If she didn't like how they were sleeping, she could just roll over. Sleep another way.

She didn't stir, so he continued. "A relationship is a decision. There's no 'supposed to' break up. There's no 'supposed to' anything, ever."

She'd had her period that night and they'd fucked first thing this morning. The skin on and around his penis was tightening as the blood dried.

"Taxes." Egypt rolled over, her face as familiar and inconceivable to him as his own. Lyle beat back the rising panic by taking her face in his hands. He needed to be grounded for the both of them.

"Taxes?"

"You're supposed to do your taxes."

Lyle understood: a provocation. Early last May, when he'd discovered that Egypt had done nothing about her taxes, not even filed for an extension, he'd been unable to veil his horror before she could latch onto it. *See*, she'd said, *you think I'm despicable.*

Edendale

"We're not talking about taxes," said Lyle.

"What are we talking about?"

"You asked if I thought we were supposed to break up."

"You didn't answer."

"I did."

"Not enough."

"I don't know what you want me to say," said Lyle. "I don't want to break up with you. Are you trying to say that you want to break up with me?"

"No."

"Then what more is there?"

"I don't know," Egypt said. "I'm sorry."

Lyle pulled her to his chest and kissed the top of her head, remembering one evening last spring when he'd stopped at the 7-Eleven on his way home from work and seen her without recognizing her. She'd been paying when he walked in and he'd absently admired her without any sense that he was looking at his girlfriend of five years—in his mind, she'd been vividly at home, waiting for him on the couch—until she turned around and said his name. Her hair had been her hair, her eyes had been her eyes, her nose, lips, and pocked forehead all undeniably hers, but in the moments after she spoke and before her features settled into the face he knew, each alien piece of her was a terrifying accusation. She'd been buying deodorant, Gatorade, and a giant bag of Sour Patch Kids.

He stroked her hair. He needed to get the sheets off or Egypt's blood would seep down onto the mattress. "It's okay," he said. "I get it. Do you see that I get it? Do you believe me?"

Ropey lifted the cat and peered into the sore. Caterpillars of puss surrounded the exposed flesh. A scab flapped loose like a mouth.

"The way I see it," said Megan, "is that, with the sore, his body is trying to tell us something. Healthy cats don't just open up like that."

Ropey tried to press the scab back over the sore but it came off in his hand. Megan produced a paper towel immediately, snatching the scab away and tossing the whole bundle in the trash.

"If he's suffering," continued Megan, "it's cruel of us to just leave him be. He has no way of getting himself care. He can't even tell us if he's in pain."

"I have the afternoon off on Wednesday. I'll take him in then."

"Wednesday?"

"Yep."

"Two days from now."

"The little dude will be fine until then." Ropey was exhausted. The tap tap tap of Egypt and Lyle's headboard against the wall above him had woken him early. "He isn't bleeding out."

"I'll just take him today after work," said Megan. "You need to call, though, and let them know that someone else is taking your cat in."

"I'm sure it's fine if you just take him."

"The vet only has your name. I'd hate to get all the way there and be turned away. And you'll need to keep your phone close by in case I need to get in touch with you."

"About what?"

"Decisions."

"I don't think anything will be that urgent."

"You don't know that."

"Fine, fine," said Ropey, cradling the cat to his shoulder. "I'll take him today before my shift."

Megan smiled and turned to leave the kitchen. She'd go upstairs and do her makeup. When she allowed, Ropey liked to sit on the closed toilet and watch: the way she changed the shape of her face with just a few powders and lotions seemed like a miracle. Today, he'd stay downstairs.

Halfway through the living room, Megan stopped. "You think I'm being ridiculous."

"Half of me does. But the other half of me knows your instincts are better than mine."

She blushed. "Thanks."

"You got it."

* * *

"I love you, too," Egypt said to Lyle, though she wanted to correct him—he couldn't love her, she took too much. But there he was, lying on his side looking at her like someone would look at a person they loved. Their room reeked of sex and period. No matter how many times he insisted it didn't bother him—he just wanted her, the blood would clean up easy—the mess of her period in their bed filled her with shame. She wanted to be pristine for him. She couldn't bear the thought of being looked at with anything but awe. He touched her shoulder and it took all her strength not to recoil. She gritted her teeth.

"What if we went on a trip?" Lyle said. His face could make her cry.

"Why would we go on a trip?"

"It could get us through whatever this is. It's a thing couples do."

"Where would we go?"

"Somewhere close."

"We can't just go on a trip."

"Why not?"

"We just can't."

"Give me one good reason why we shouldn't go on a trip," Lyle said, "besides that you're feeling sad right now."

Edendale

"I don't want to." She didn't know why she said it. She'd like very much to go on a trip with Lyle. And they'd go, whether she agreed to it now or later. Egypt held no illusions of control. The world would do what it wanted with her. Soon, Lyle would lift the sheet, revealing her menstrual blood drying on his stomach, groin, and thighs. Her stomach flipped. She wanted to swaddle herself in dark rags and lock every door against him.

"Okay, we don't have to go."

"Thank you," said Egypt, but now she was desolate, realizing she'd wanted him to fight back. Force her. Lyle rose from the bed. It was worse than she thought. His entire front side, from belly button to mid-thigh, seemed sponge-painted red and brown. His pubic hair was matted with her blood, and the small curl of brown clot clung to his tired dick. He saw her looking.

"It's okay. I don't think it's gross. You're my girlfriend. I love every part of you."

The bathroom door locked from the inside. Egypt heard the clatter of Megan's make-up kit on the sink and caught the moment of panic on Lyle's face as he looked to the closed bathroom door, then the bedside clock. Megan's routine was long; now Lyle would either have to arrive late to work or spend the day caked with dried menstrual blood beneath his suit. She watched him swallow the panic down for her sake. He took his towel off the back of the door, dipped it in the glass of water he kept by the bed, and started dabbing at his stomach. So he'd leave for work on time. Now, it would be up to Egypt to soak the sheets, and though she knew that cold water took out blood, that you just had to get them in as fast as you could, she also knew that she wouldn't.

The air purifier whirred on.

"That thing is so fucking loud," Egypt said. "It keeps waking me up."

Lyle unplugged it.

"Sorry, love," he said.

2.

The vet clamped one blue latex hand on Captain America's throat, wrapping the other around the back of his neck to prevent the cat from backing away. Her face was serious but kind, with brushed hair and clean, bare skin. Ropey imagined she'd been the kind of girl who sat in the front of the school bus with her book bag secure in her lap. She'd have done her homework promptly upon arriving home, spending the rest of the afternoon out with the horses, nuzzling their wet snouts and scraping the muck from their hooves. As she examined his cat, Ropey began to feel insecure. He imagined that she could read Captain America's health like a tarot card, seeing the ways he'd failed as a cat owner in each fatty organ or scrape of tartar.

"Put your finger here," she said to Ropey.

"Here?"

"No, here." The vet guided Ropey's finger to a jellybean mound attached to the left side of the cat's trachea. "Feel that?"

"I feel it." Ropey pressed and the jellybean slid away, retreating deeper into the cat's interior.

"And this?" she lifted Ropey's finger and placed it on a much larger mound attached to the other side of Captain America's trachea. This mound was spongy, bulbous. Ropey traced its hills and valleys, finding a hard spot like a little seed. He wiggled the seed and the mound convulsed around it. Captain America yelped and struggled backward. His nails slipped on the metal examination table. Ropey, horrified, pulled his offending hand to his chest, holding it there with the other.

"Easy." The vet stroked Captain America's back. "Easy, boy."

"Sorry," said Ropey, but the vet had already moved on, releasing Captain America so she could scribble something in his file. Ropey hoped that this was because wiggling the seed wasn't too grave an offense. He scolded himself for needing the vet's approval. Still, his mind filled with scenarios in which she expressed her admiration. She'd tell him stories about her worst clients, lamenting that more pet owners weren't like him—sensitive yet practical when confronted with their animal's pain—as she walked him to the door, as she called him with Captain America's lab results, as they sipped foam off their lagers in a shaded beer garden recalling the day they fell in love.

Edendale

Free to roam wherever he pleased, Captain America slunk to the back of the examination table and pressed his face against the wall.

"Those are Captain America's thyroids," said the vet. "You felt the inflammation on the right? I'll need to run a blood test to confirm, but his symptoms are pretty standard for hyperthyroidism."

"It's bad?" Ropey felt like a fool.

"Untreated, hyperthyroidism is terminal in cats. The lesions are probably a result of excessive scratching or rubbing—this condition causes overactivity in a lot of cats—but they could also indicate a food or seasonal allergy. We'll monitor. For the hyperthyroidism, we have three treatment options."

As the vet explained these options, Ropey admired her healthy teeth. Suddenly, he remembered a tall stranger in a floral dress bending down to scold him for running up a slide. The slide had been metal, hot on his bare shins each time he slid down. He could not place the woman. She was not his mother, not the mother of a friend, not a teacher or a babysitter. She must have been twelve feet tall.

"I don't recommend anesthesia for a cat in his condition," said the vet. "Which leaves us with the hormone ointment and the radioactive iodine treatment. The ointment would mask the symptoms and prevent further damage, but only if administered every twelve hours, precisely. It's a tough schedule to keep. The radiation is just a one-time thing, and it kills the tumor for good."

"How long would he need to stay on the ointment for?"

"The rest of his life."

Ropey massaged the cat between the ears. The vet continued to explain. After the iodine injection, Captain America would be highly radioactive for over a week. He'd be kept in a special metal crate at the veterinary hospital for ten to fifteen days and fed through a slot in the wall. Cats undergoing radioactive iodine treatment were allowed one comfort object for their crate. She recommended a cotton shirt or a small towel that smelled of home.

"Afterwards, the comfort object will need to be incinerated, so it's best not to choose anything too sentimental."

Ropey nodded.

"Any questions?"

"This is all if the tests come back positive, right?"

"The tests are really just for confirmation."

On the walk home, Captain America wailed mournfully. Coyotes aside, Ropey imagined that the cat wanted at least one more jaunt outside before death or serious medical intervention. In his situation, Ropey certainly would. He hummed the Star-Spangled Banner, trying to calm him. They cut through the Rite Aid parking lot.

"We saw a guy beat up a chick, here," Ropey told the cat.

The cat shifted back and forth, rocking the carrier.

"I know, man. The worst is, after he left, Lyle kept trying to figure out if the guy been telling the truth about them dating, like that was a crux of the situation. Dude dragged her across the lot."

At the base of Lemoyne, Ropey lowered the carrier to the gravel shoulder and unzipped Captain America's door.

"Okay, okay. Just be careful. Promise you'll come home when you're done, okay, bud?"

The cat walked out of the carrier and wound a figure eight around Ropey's legs. He looked up at him, meowed showing all his pointed teeth, then tiptoed back into the carrier and settled down, waiting for Ropey to close the door.

"Well," said Ropey. "Well."

3.

"The iodine would cure him completely?" Megan asked Ropey as she shuffled through the folder of glossy pamphlets he'd brought home from the vet. Lyle stood at her shoulder, reading along, and Ropey paced the kitchen, vigorously rubbing his mouth. Egypt watched them all. She felt danger in the room, swelling like a thunderhead. She pulled her knees to her chest. Sealed her mouth.

"The iodine," repeated Megan. "It's low risk and nearly one hundred percent effective? Am I reading this wrong?"

"Yeah, I think that's what the vet was saying." Ropey looked over at Egypt. She felt his glance like a rod through her chest. "But the sores might actually be from allergies or something? She also said he can't have the surgery. He isn't healthy enough for anesthesia."

"Then it's obvious, right?" asked Megan.

Ropey said nothing. His hand grew violent over his mouth.

"Wait, there's the ointment, too," said Lyle.

"That just masks the symptoms? Did I misunderstand?" Since Egypt had known her, Megan argued in questions. Egypt, whose rent are we missing? Egypt, what do you know about the door being unlocked? Upstairs, Captain America was a lump under Megan's quilt where he'd been hiding since Ropey had brought him home from the vet.

Lyle took the pamphlet from Megan's hands. "You're talking about the radioactive iodine therapy? It's twelve hundred dollars."

"What are you saying?" asked Megan.

"That twelve hundred dollars is a lot of money," said Lyle.

"The disease is terminal untreated," said Megan.

"He's not a young cat," said Lyle. "We have to consider how many years he has left in him. What if we paid for this now and then he had a heart attack in a few months?"

"My god," said Megan. "He's a cat, not an investment."

Egypt disliked them both very much in the moment; Megan determined to prove herself good and Lyle determined to prove, what? His frugality? There was an image of a woman in a white lab coat on the front of the pamphlet Lyle was holding. Her blond hair was pulled into an elegant twist, her stethoscope draped over her neck. She held the ear of a golden retriever aloft to smile into his dark canal.

Megan snatched the pamphlet back. "He can't have the surgery and the ointment only treats the symptoms. So it's the only real option. I'll call the vet. Maybe there's some kind of payment plan. Ropey, I'll help. I have savings. You know I'll help, right?"

Ropey walked to the window above the sink, put a stick of incense in the mouth of the porcelain frog, and lit its fragrant end.

"Ropey?" Megan repeated. "How does that sound?"

Egypt had painted the frog herself at a storefront studio in North Hollywood. It was a gift for Megan: an apology for giving her lice. The only other customers that day were attending a sixth birthday party. One girl had kept wandering over to criticize Egypt's work—frogs don't have boobs!—and to steal each of her paint brushes, one by one.

"I wish I could talk with the little dude about it," Ropey said to the porcelain frog.

"I'm also thinking," continued Lyle, "if he's hiding after an hour at the vet, how is a ten-day radiation treatment going to affect him?"

"He'll hide for a bit. And then he'll stop hiding. And then he won't die."

"Everything dies, Megan," said Lyle.

"Jesus. Yes, we will all eventually die. Congratulations, Lyle. You are so enlightened. Now that you're done educating us, can we talk about our sick cat?"

"That's my point," said Lyle. "We're talking about expensive medical interventions for a cat."

"Captain America," said Megan.

"Who is a cat," said Lyle.

"Who is also our friend who has a curable disease but no means to seek treatment on his own because he is a cat." Megan slammed her hand down on the counter. Her chest heaved.

"Who is old," said Lyle. He spoke low and steady. "Who has lived a full life."

"Twelve is not that old," said Megan.

Egypt watched Ropey take up another pamphlet. The cat on the front of this one looked stuffed, eyeballs made of glass.

"Ropey's sick cat," she said.

"Look who finally woke up," said Megan.

"I'm correcting you." Egypt sat up straight. "Ropey's sick cat. Not ours. Not either of yours."

Megan covered her face. "Ropey," she said through her hands, "I'd be happy to give your cat that ointment in perfect twelve-hour intervals so long as we're still living together, if that's the route you choose."

"I need to think," said Ropey.

"Please, let me give him the ointment, at least until you make a decision," she said. "For his comfort. I'll pay for everything. I'll do everything."

Lyle placed his hand on Megan's shoulder. She jerked away. "Don't touch me," she said, and Lyle remained there, his rejected hand hovering out in front of him. It began to shake. His face scrunched up. And though Egypt felt the same disgust for him that she saw all over Megan's face, she also felt herself standing up, walking across the kitchen, and taking Lyle by that hovering hand. She led him out into the yard. She sat him down on one of their ratty lounge chairs and snuggled up beside him. She put the hand on her lap, petting it.

"Just trying to have a conversation," he was saying, "Just trying to weigh all the possibilities."

Egypt watched Megan and Ropey's silent conversation through the sliding glass doors. Megan persisted. Ropey shook his head, worked his hands through his beard, then finally shrugged, a surrender.

"Like I'm some kind of monster," Lyle was saying. Egypt didn't respond. Instead, she pet and pet and pet. Once, Lyle came down with a 24-hour flu so violent that each time he vomited the pressure made him shit, and each time he shit the smell made him vomit. Always resourceful, he parked himself on their toilet with a trashcan between his knees, apologizing to the rest of them through the closed doors. When he was finally empty, he crawled from the bathroom to their bedroom floor, where he collapsed. His cheeks were red, his eyes were bright and glassy, and as Egypt stood above him, swimming in the stench of his illness, she found his new complexion attractive. She cleaned the bathroom while he slept, using up two whole rolls of paper towels.

"Oh? Could you not find the rags?" Megan had scolded when she saw what Egypt had done. "But thank you."

Now, the sky was thick, the wind hot. Their tree was so swollen with ripe lemons that it seemed branches would start crashing to the ground. Egypt watched Megan and Ropey leave the kitchen. She felt Lyle, in all his sadness. He was a real, live human. Beside her.

"Let's go on a trip," she said.

"Really?"

"Yes."

"I'll start looking into places," said Lyle. His face brightened with excitement. "Don't worry, I'll make it as cheap as I can. Unless you want to plan. Do you want to help with the planning? Do you mind if it's a surprise?"

"No. Surprise me."

4.

In early October, Lyle began to test it. Not out loud, not to anyone he knew, barely even to himself.

I'm going to propose to my girlfriend next week, he said in his head to the man selling him his lunchtime snow cone.

For my fiancée, he imagined himself telling the woman behind the counter at the dry cleaners as he handed her Egypt's yellow dress. *See this tear. Can you fix it?*

We're honeymooning in France, he thought at the man in the fancy wine shop. *Figured we should try to get a taste for things, first.* He was nauseous with excitement. Lyle had always known that he would someday be a man proposing to a woman, seeing himself and his future wife shrouded in a dreamy fog. Their faces were fuzzy, their silhouettes made generic by distance and convention: the world was so full of husbands and wives that they all seemed to blend together. Man

Edendale

shape. Woman shape. But now that this idea had struck him—it could be Egypt, the man could be him and the woman, her—his wife was rushing forward, filling in. Lyle gripped the bottle like contraband on the way out to his car. The wine was not, in fact, from France, but they'd drink it anyways.

5.

When the school day finally ended, Megan helped her students into their backpacks, sent them waddling off with their guardians, and flicked off the classroom lights. Her pulse thudded in her temples. She'd lashed out. She'd overstepped. Still, a sick cat should be treated. Megan closed her eyes. As a child, she'd been terrified of her soft spots. What if she accidentally pressed? Now, she gave her temples a deep rub. Being an adult had its advantages.

Someone knocked on her open classroom door.

"Ms. Bell?" A pretty woman craned her neck in, squinting against the dark. Megan spun through her mental Rolodex of students' parents. This was Lucas's mother. Holly? Hailey? "Ms. Bell, can I steal a minute of your time?"

"Absolutely." Megan put on her best smile and straightened her skirt. Lucas was a small, energetic boy with bad manners. He sought physical affection constantly, pressing into Megan whenever she knelt down beside him. Though he came to school each morning smelling like soap and sunscreen, he emitted a sharp, chemical odor by two o'clock dismissal. Holly, Megan decided. Holly wore a sleek pair of overalls and carried her phone and keys in her hand instead of in a purse. She was alone, as a nanny had picked Lucas up from dismissal.

Megan gestured toward the art table. She and Holly each pulled out a miniature chair.

"Lucas is beside himself," Holly said. "Something about a book?"

Yesterday, Lucas had refused to return *The Big Book of Carnivores* to the classroom library, claiming he'd handed it directly to her sometime before. This was his third strike, as *The Big Book of Engines* and *Bones in Your Backyard* had also disappeared while in his possession. Megan had sent home her standard note.

"I'm sorry to hear that his consequence upset him. Lucas will be able to borrow books from the Story Center again in four weeks. I'll send home another note when the time comes. This doesn't affect his school library privileges at all. I explained this to him but I'd be happy to go back over it if he's feeling anxious about not having enough reading material. Does your family use the public library?"

"Of course."

"Excellent. Lucas has a wonderful appetite for books."

Holly sucked in her lips. The mother wasn't done.

"Your son is such an enthusiastic reader," Megan said. "It's clear that literacy has an important place in your home."

"He's not upset about losing his library privileges."

"Oh?" Megan had guessed this much.

"I'm just trying to piece together what happened. Lucas seems to believe that you called him a liar. Of course, I know you wouldn't say that, but I'm guessing that he felt—wrongly, of course—that you felt that way because of how the situation unfolded. He's distraught. He's sure that he handed you the book and he's frustrated you won't entertain his version of the situation. My husband and I put a very strong emphasis on always telling the truth, so Lucas finds it upsetting to be accused of not telling it."

Megan's preschoolers loved to lie—most had just discovered the handy trick—and Lucas was the biggest liar in her classroom.

"Thanks so much for bringing this to my attention."

Holly brightened. "I knew it was a misunderstanding."

"It's important that Lucas feels loved and trusted in the classroom, so this is something I want to address immediately."

"I've gone through our entire house. The book isn't there."

Sure it was. Megan pushed on. "I'd normally go about solving a problem like this by taking special care to acknowledge Lucas's honesty for the next few days." Megan paused, studying Holly's reaction. The mother had picked her phone and keys up off the table. "For example, when he tells the truth about something, I'll pause for a moment and say 'Lucas, I see you're telling the truth.'"

Megan watched Holly's mind flit away to something else, probably dinner, an appointment, whatever she had planned for the night, and knew she'd satisfied her. Most parents didn't need to get their way. They just needed to engage with her enough to stave off the guilt.

After Holly left, Megan wiped down the tables and chairs, the thud in her temples decreasing with each sticky print annihilated, and gathered her things. Someone had left a bowl of backyard oranges in the teachers' room. Megan shoved a few in her bag on the way out, tangle of leaves and woody stems still attached. In the playground, Holly stood in animated conversation with her nanny as Lucas played with April, another preschooler. The children stood face to face on the rope bridge, taking turns demonstrating dance moves. As Megan passed the playground, Holly lit up and waved, her enthusiasm prompting the nanny to turn and see Megan also. The nanny waved, and Megan waved back at both of them. The children then paused their game to join in, each waving with both hands while jumping up and down on the rope bridge. The bridge swayed. Megan copied the children, jumping and waving with both hands, her hair going wild and her bag full of oranges smacking against her side. The children doubled over in giggles. How funny Ms. Bell could be.

6.

"Egypt." Ropey took a long gulp of water to center himself. They were out back on the ratty lounge chairs, Ropey in cotton shorts and Egypt in a bikini that she kept untying and retying, shifting around the small triangles of fabric and pooling the strings on top. "Did you borrow anything from my room, lately?"

It was very hot and the yard stunk of rotting citrus and wildfire, but Ropey had joined Egypt in the sun because he believed that he could help her. He placed his sweating glass down onto the cement slab between their chairs. Inside the sliding doors, Captain America stood on his thin hind legs with his front paws up against the glass. Egypt was so pale. She'd burn, she was already burning.

"Could you be more specific?"

"I'm missing some money."

"No, I didn't borrow any of your money."

"I don't want this to seem like an ambush. I'm not accusing you. I'm not even angry."

She took his water and touched the sweating glass against her forehead, holding her bikini top to her chest as she bent forward. "This sun," she said. "Is it even noon?"

Ropey had a policy against making theories about people. He'd once lived in a house where everyone but him was writing a screenplay or a novel. These want-to-be writers, they'd get drunk and then go on and on about one another's personalities: analyzing, characterizing, and filing away. The whole thing disgusted him. People needed space to shift and expand.

"Talk to me," he said.

Egypt turned onto her side, showing him the sharp bones of her back.

"Well, did you have it after you brought that girl home? She's the only stranger that any of us have had in the house, recently."

"Lisa?"

"I'd forgotten it was Lisa."

"You didn't forget that it was Lisa."

The cat banged against the door with the top of his head, rattling the glass in its frame.

"We need to have a conversation," Ropey said.

"What are we doing right now?" Egypt rolled onto her back and arched, toes pointing. The bikini slid. Ropey saw nipple and averted his eyes.

"Don't do that," said Ropey.

"Don't do what?"

"You know," said Ropey.

She said nothing. She was so young. Her freckled skin was burning. He pictured her tiptoeing into his room, pulling out his dresser drawer, taking out the box and skimming a five off the top. The room was static gray from the closed blinds, darkening when his tapestry door swung closed behind her. It wasn't his job to understand, but to love despite. Because sometimes there is no understanding. Because the others will try to understand.

Ropey sat upright on his lounge chair. He swung his feet around and placed them on the ground, facing Egypt. Somewhere in the neighborhood, a baby cried through an open window. The cat paced the length of the sliding door.

"If you're having problems with money, I can lend you some." Ropey waited, watching her work to keep her face steady. "I'm not going to tell Megan or Lyle about this. I don't even want it back. I'm telling you that I can see that you're suffering, and that I'm here. Talk to me. Or just talk to someone."

Ropey took another long gulp of water to give her time. He'd given his speech. It was lame, so lame. He got up off the lounge. Soft lemons littered the ground around the tree. He rolled one beneath the arch of his left foot. Relax the body, relax the mind. He switched the lemon to his right arch. Lately, Megan always seemed to be scurrying around beneath the tree, trying to gather up the lemons to use them before they rotted. He admired how she panicked at the prospect of waste. It seemed to indicate some kind of virtue. The tree stood outside his bedroom window, right above his head, and he could hear her out there on mornings when he slept late. She wafted into his dreams, her arms growing long and woody, her gnarled hands reaching through his blinds to drop her plump ripe fruit into his bed.

Egypt pressed the skin of her shoulder. "I'm going inside," she said. "I think I'm starting to burn."

"Do you owe Lyle money?"

"Does that excite you?"

It did. Ropey squashed the lemon beneath his foot. The juice ran into the cuts on his toes. He'd always thought of them as ten jolly little men. The nails were their faces, the knuckles their happy hairy bellies. Now he saw them for who they really were. Lecherous little fucks. Go ahead, he thought, wiggling them around in the yellow-brown pulp. He felt his ugly intentions suddenly exposed. He'd hoped to be a rubber point in the triangle, deflecting Egypt back to Lyle. But instead here he was, another man trying to crack open a woman so he could slurp up her yolk.

"I'm sorry," he said, but even that felt like a manipulation.

"I'm going inside." She left the door open behind her. "Go," she said to the cat, but, with the door open, Captain America was no longer interested in the yard. "Go." The cat turned and followed Egypt inside.

7.

Lyle often found it difficult to focus on things that weren't Egypt. To be productive at work, he'd designated a section of his brain—back left, tucked up against the hard curve of his skull—her home. Whenever she emerged front and center in his thoughts, he visualized a miniature version of himself taking a miniature version of her by the wrist, leading her over the gray terrain, and latching her in.

Now, there were one hundred and three unread emails in his inbox and an actor on line five who couldn't figure out where to park. The agent wanted her Diet Coke, but there were no Diet Cokes in the fridge. Though Lyle had needed to pee for the past two hours, he took breaks only when the agent did. He was trying to move up. Assistant to Coordinator to Junior Agent to Agent. His mind cycled over this path at least once every hour.

Lyle navigated the actor to the correct studio lot, answering the ten most urgent emails as he read out rights and lefts. The agent called for her Diet Coke again.

Edendale

"Cover my desk for five?" Lyle asked the assistant across the hall. Alone in the elevator, he closed his eyes, let her out. Hi, Egypt. She was in their bed. She was walking through their yard. She was sitting on the front steps, watching the cars come down the hill. There was the clammy skin beneath her bent knee. There was the sweet corner of her mouth. The floor below had no Diet Cokes. Neither did the next, or the next. On the ride down to the stockroom, Lyle checked his phone and discovered four missed calls from the same, unsaved number. He called it back. A man picked up.

"Hi, I just got four missed calls from this number?"

Silence, then: "Oh, some girl used my phone a few hours ago. Skinny chick with a bad sunburn? Huge Dodgers shirt? At first I thought she wasn't wearing any shorts, but her shirt was just covering them."

Egypt. Why was she calling him from some random guy's phone? How had the shorts eventually been revealed?

"Was she hurt?" Lyle asked instead.

"No, just really sunburned. She said she was lost and her phone was dead. Seemed chill, though."

"Where was this?"

"Like Venice and La Brea? Or around there. She knocked on my car window while I was stopped at a light."

"Is she still there?" Lyle pushed down the mild panic. She was an adult. The world was relatively safe.

"I don't know, dude. Sorry. I'm miles away now."

In the stockroom, Lyle stuffed a Diet Coke into each of his pockets thinking of Egypt, sunburned, in that tee-shirt cannon shirt. She'd slept in it last night and would probably sleep in it again tonight. Lyle suppressed a shiver. He believed that people should have separate day clothes and night clothes. There was filth; there were smells; there were dried out bits of rice and cheese always stuck to the fronts of Egypt's shirts. When he'd left her in bed this morning, her skin had been its typical freckly pale. Now, she was sunburned and a three-hour walk from home. It struck him that he might never see her again. Without a phone or car, Egypt could drift away like a boat cut loose from its mooring.

In the elevator on the way up, he tried Megan and Ropey. Neither answered. He shook away an image of Egypt tripping along a dusty curb. When he brought the agent her Coke, she looked up from her desk.

"Something's wrong," she said.

Lyle moved to take back the Diet Coke.

"No, with you. You look like you just shot your mother."

For the first time, it occurred to Lyle that he could leave work, go to her. This realization crumbled his wall.

Edendale

The panic rose up. She was not in the bed. She was not watching the cars come down the hill. It wasn't normal to be so worried about an adult in the world. But she wasn't an adult. She was his fragile little rodent. His barely embodied angel.

"Egypt was in an accident." He winced as he said it. Lying was the only transgression for which his father would get out the stick.

"Oh my god, do you need to go? Of course you need to go. I'm making you go. Take the rest of the day off or you're fired."

8.

He didn't find her at Venice and La Brea. Not a block away in any direction, either. Though he knew her phone was dead, he called her repeatedly as he drove wider rectangles around the grid. Each strip mall lined block seemed identical. Bright, grimy signs advertised transmission repair, checks cashed here, and donuts for ninety-nine cents. The wide sky pressed the city flat and there were few trees to temper the sun. In the heat, pedestrians hurried to and from their cars, squinting up to check the regulations on the parking signs.

Ropey called him back.

"She was still at the house when I left for work," he told Lyle.

"Did she mention anywhere she was going today?"

"She didn't."

"Could she be on anything?"

"No. Or, maybe we smoked a little this morning? Nothing that would, like, disorient her though. Unless she's been holding out on us."

Edendale

"Right. Cool. Thanks."

A moment of tension. Ropey breathing in and out. Lyle could almost see his cracked lips. The white forest of his tongue. He felt something coming. His fingers tightened around the steering wheel.

"What?" Lyle asked.

"Egypt and I argued earlier today."

"What about?"

"I'm sorry, man. I promised I wouldn't tell. I mean, the details won't point you to a location or anything. Just, she was upset. I upset her."

Lyle hung up politely and drove a few blocks without breathing, blood rushing to his face. Egypt and Ropey, arguing about something he wasn't allowed to know. He thought about Egypt, not his Egypt, but Egypt a woman, out in the world. She had conversations that he was not part of. She ran private errands, saw and heard things that she never relayed back. He imagined her leaning into that man's car window, asking if she could use his phone. He'd never hear the voice she used when he wasn't around. He'd never see how she held her shoulders, the way she set her lips.

Megan called back.

"Have you been asking around?" she asked. "Are you showing people her picture?" She told him that she'd head back to the house in case Egypt returned, demanding that he call her with any news.

Lyle pulled over in a fifteen-minute zone and scrolled through his camera roll, searching for the right picture of Egypt. He had her doing handstands, her displaying mouthfuls of food, one of her pulling her foot all the way up over her head. He settled on a picture of her posing in front of a wall of graffiti. In it, she looked grumpy and overheated, which was how he assumed she looked right now. When he looked up from his phone, he was startled to see her right across the street. Egypt sat on a sunny bus stop bench. She held her knees to her chest with her shirt pulled down over them. She squinted against the sun. Behind the bench, a palm tree cast a slim strip of shade. Lyle felt a wave of frustration: why wasn't she waiting in the shade? He scrambled out of his car and crossed the street. She waved. His heart surged.

"What are you doing here?" she asked.

"What? You called me," said Lyle. "You're lost."

"I'm not lost. I'm waiting for this bus."

First, Lyle became angry with the man he'd spoken to on the phone. That liar, he thought. What a prank to pull. But as that flash of anger subsided, he looked at Egypt. Her knees stuck up through the neck of her shirt like some kind of cartoon cleavage. Her eyes were red, her dirty face tear-streaked. There was no configuration of reality in which the liar was the man on the phone.

Edendale

In every configuration of reality, the woman he wanted to marry lied quite a bit. Lyle's head became unbearably heavy. He sat on the bench beside her to cradle it in his hands.

"Where can I take you right now?" he asked.
"Nowhere."
"Egypt, where are you trying to go?"
"This is my bus."
"I left work. I can drive you."
"I'm sorry you left work. I didn't ask you to."
"That's not what I meant."
"Of course it was."

This wasn't fair; he'd built his career around hers, but he reached for her arm in apology anyways. She scooted away.

"On days you need my car," he tried, "you can drop me at work and take it. Or I can find a ride."

"That's my bus, you can go."

Lyle didn't see a bus. "I'll drive you to wherever you're trying to get to."

"Lyle, let me take the bus. I want to take the bus."

They were thirty-five minutes from home via car. On a city bus, it would probably take close to two hours. There might not be air-conditioning. There would be old people with carts and carts of groceries. Lyle began to walk back to the car. "This is ridiculous," he said, but Egypt did not follow.

In the car, Lyle turned on the air-conditioning and waited, watching Egypt on her bench. She didn't look in his direction. She didn't go into the shade. Egypt was stubborn, her aggressive side woven into her passivity. The bus finally pulled up in front of her, sighing as it knelt toward the sidewalk. On its side, there was an advertisement for cool sculpting that showed four torsos: two male and two female, two fat and dimpled and two reddened but toned. When the bus pulled away, Egypt remained on the bench. Though he'd won, Lyle felt a tinge of disappointment. He couldn't help but root for her. He started the car, did a U-turn in the street, and stopped in front of her. She got in.

"Where am I taking you?" asked Lyle.

"Home."

"Oh. Where are you coming from, then?" Lyle asked.

"Home."

"But where were you trying to go? I can take you there."

"Home. Just home."

Lyle drove. Los Angeles, endless, unknowable, was just a map. Not like his hometown, where, even now, he could travel down each road in his mind. All the dead ends and cul-de-sacs were filled in, full color. He'd been down this street for a pool party in seventh grade. This one to drop off a coworker the summer after he graduated from high school. Los Angeles was for Egypt. He'd always told her that he could live anywhere with air, work, light, and her.

"I know I'm not being fair to you," she said. "I'm using you like a guinea pig."

"You're not using me."

"I certainly am."

"How?"

"I could tell you what this is all about," she offered.

"Only if you want to." He didn't want her to.

"I was unsure if I was actually capable of choosing to do something. I thought maybe I was just a passenger. So I chose something and I did it."

There were problems with this logic. What if her choice was just another part of the stream? Also, she was lying. Either to him or herself. She'd run away because she'd fought with Ropey. Lyle thought it best not to point either of these things out. He drove on. After a while, they stopped at a red light in front of a strip mall where, in front of a Smog Checks Here sign, there was a plywood outbuilding in the parking lot selling stonework. Garden angels, pet gravestones, birdbaths, pavers. Lyle noted the absence of human gravestones and wondered if this was because making them required a special permit. Or maybe it just didn't make sense to carve up prototypes, as each family's desires were probably pretty specific. He turned to Egypt. She sat slumped with her ear against the car window, eyes half closed.

"Look at all those birdbaths," he said in his most cheerful voice.

9.

Years before, when a private foundation announced a mission to establish permanent human life on Mars, Egypt applied to be part of the first wave of settlers. This was after college, but before the house on Lemoyne Street, when she and Megan were still moving from sublet to sublet up in the valley. For her application, Egypt recorded a video essay, filled out a long medical questionnaire, then waited, telling no one about her application. The secret gave her energy. Her Martian future spread fresh and open: a clean, shining plane. A few months later, Egypt received a short email from the foundation. *Dear Ms. Muldoon, We regret to inform you . . .*

Those who made it through to the second round were doctors, athletes, concert musicians: people with something to contribute to the new civilization on Mars. Not Egypt, useless Egypt, whose shoes were all falling apart.

Now, the remaining candidates were about to move into the mouth of a dormant volcano somewhere in the Pacific. Their task: survival. They'd build a village of fiberglass igloos and grow vegetables without using soil. They'd bounce around in spacesuits and tease potable water straight from the air. After two years in Los Angeles, Egypt didn't feel like surviving anymore. She wanted to sleep. She wanted close all the windows, pull the sheets up over her head, and zonk out for days and days and days.

10.

Megan entered the living room where her three roommates were passing the bong around an unfinished puzzle and announced that she was sorry about the other night, she'd overstepped. Could she make it up to them by cooking a big dinner?

"The cat," she explained when all three looked blankly back.

"Make up for it?" asked Ropey.

"I overstepped," she said again.

"Oh, it's cool," said Ropey, "I asked your opinion."

"But still. The way I argued. I shouldn't lose my shit like that."

Lyle beamed at her, nodding, and Megan blossomed open. She knelt beside the coffee table to join work on the puzzle. For Megan, puzzles could be dangerous. Their promise transfixed her. She'd find herself dry-mouthed and exhausted above the completed thing long after she'd meant to go to bed, dissatisfaction spidering through her despite each piece being in its rightful place. The jumble had been sorted, disorder conquered with diligence and time. So where was the relief?

This puzzle, when completed, would be a black and white photograph of a sea of mini M&M's. Lyle had picked it up as a joke—what kind of people would torture themselves with such a ridiculous task?—yet here she was, bent over the coffee table with her roommates, attempting to solve it anyways.

"So, is everyone around next Wednesday night?" Megan asked. "For dinner?"

"Yes," said Lyle.

"Yes," said Ropey.

"Sure," said Egypt, as Lyle rubbed aloe into the back of her neck.

11.

Ropey cleared off the top of his dresser, placed his money box in the center, and propped it open. If he was offering it, maybe it wouldn't have the same effect. He paced out into the kitchen, back into his room, then back through the kitchen and out into the dark yard. The sky blinked. The night chirped. Ropey decided that the whole setup would just fan the flames and went back into his room to hide the money again.

12.

The house was still. Egypt, in bed, was not sleeping. Not tonight, not ever again, she feared.

A sheeted ridge beside her, Lyle's sleeping body seemed empty, just a husk, all his Lyle-ness gone out with his consciousness, leaving this pile of dumb flesh behind. There was no Lyle there. And so what was she? Egypt's own body felt very loud and very angry, the way a boil must feel on an otherwise serene face. She wanted to sleep. She wanted him to wake. She wanted, something. The husk breathed the easy rhythmic breathing of any body, at rest. Egypt got out of bed, drifted through the dark bathroom, and, after looming over Megan's bed for a long moment, lifted the sheet and slipped in.

Lying awake beside a sleeping Megan was not so different than lying awake beside a sleeping Lyle. The torment of serene breath, the husk beneath the sheet. Egypt throbbed. She felt that if she had to survive one more minute alone, she'd dissipate.

Edendale

"Hi there," said Megan's voice in the dark, and Egypt began to weep.

Megan sat up and turned on the light.

"Here's what we're going to do," said Megan. "We're going to get you some more money, fill up your time. I want you to force yourself to meet people. Go to at least one audition per week. Join a sketch team. Have you considered babysitting? A bunch of my kids' nannies act. This is about money and time. That's it. That's all we need to fix. You and Lyle are perfect together. I know—I've been here the whole time. Can you pick up any more shifts at Little Wink? Small adjustments, Egypt. That's it. I promise. And how do you think babysitting sounds?"

13.

The next afternoon, Megan helped Egypt set up a profile online. The profile worked: two days later a woman with three daughters called.

"Are you available this coming Wednesday afternoon from one to five?"

Egypt was scheduled for the lunch shift at Little Wink on Wednesdays. She told the woman so.

"Any other day," Egypt said, feeling the ribbon slip through her fingers. Up, up, and away. "My schedule is so, so open! Just not Wednesday afternoons. Please hold onto my number. Call me if anything else comes up!"

14.

On Wednesday, at 11:30 a.m., Lisa called.

"Slow day," she said. "It's the smoke. Do you want the afternoon off?"

"Not really," said Egypt. "Things are a little tight."

"Well, we have to cut someone, and you're the only person on the schedule who isn't here yet. I'll make a note that, if anyone is looking for a sub this week, they should call you first."

Egypt did not call the woman with three daughters, sure she'd already found someone else. She did not call Megan, either. When the sadness began to ink out from the center of her belly, Egypt tore herself from the house (Who had built this bungalow to be so shady? Who had forgotten that humans, like plants, need sunlight and air?) and fled down Lemoyne onto Sunset, where she took refuge from the heat at her bank. The bank was old, marble, cavernous. Since she was there, she got in line. Since she made it to the front of the line, she walked up to the next available teller. The teller was her age, female, seemed all in one piece. Could the two of them be friends? Could Egypt become a bank teller, too? But the teller had no style. She wore polyester dress pants that flared at the bottom and had flat-ironed her hair. It hung so close to her face! Egypt looked down at her own outfit, thinking it would inspire envy and realized she was still in one of Lyle's tee shirts. It was holey, hanging off her like a sack. She knotted the shirt at the waist, but, though this improved the top half of her silhouette, it also revealed that her jeans—Megan's jeans, actually—were belted with a shoelace.

"I'd like to close my account," Egypt said.

"Oh, you can't do that at this window. You have to make an appointment with one of our personal advisors." The teller gestured over to a cluster of desks behind a full waiting area. "Walk-ins can sign in and wait for the next available advisor."

"Can I just withdraw everything from my account, then?"

The teller looked at her screen and did some clicking around. "For your account, you need to keep a minimum of ten or you'll be charged a fee."

"Okay, then I'll just take out as much as I can."

The teller clicked around some more. "And how would you like your $97.63?"

Edendale

"Ones."

Egypt left cradling her little white envelope of cash. If she imagined the bills were fifties, hundreds it felt thick enough. Down the block, a salon advertised a midday special on pedicures, so Egypt wandered in, breathing deep the smell of acrylic. A woman led her to a big pleather chair. Powered on, the chair went at Egypt's back with all its fists. She watched the pedicurist work her feet with envy. What precision, what speed. Egypt's broken chalk skin regained its peach, became glossy with moisture. Each toenail transformed into a perfect, purple stone. Megan once told her that she should be grateful for all the privilege she'd had even though it was now gone. But it ruined my personality, she'd said back, and Megan hadn't argued.

Egypt tipped the pedicurist one hundred percent and then let her shining new feet take her and her ruined personality wherever they wanted. Hello, Little Wink. The pedicured feet carried her across the lush, tree-shaded patio, in past the checkered tablecloths, to the bar. The restaurant was, in fact, dead. Ropey polished wine glasses behind the empty bar. His face lit with enthusiasm when he saw her. He liked her. It meant so much to be liked. Saddling up on a stool, she thought of being in his room alone. Of the pleasure of sorting money. Of counting it, of counting it again.

Lisa appeared. She laughed nervously at Egypt's presence. Her discomfort seemed sincere. Egypt felt all swishy inside. Like she was holding things that didn't belong. If someone would only cut her open right now. Released, her guts could slide to the ground like those of a fish.

"I know," said Egypt to Lisa, "I'm not here to work. I'm just very lonely. Will you guys drink with me?"

Egypt bought each of them a beer, then another beer, then a shot before her envelope was empty. Drunk, she kept reaching down to feel her toes. She loved the grease the pedicurist had put on them. It made her look perfect from her ankle down, like she was made of wax. She pulled her leg up above the bar, spread her toes, and lectured Ropey and Lisa about self-care. When it became obvious that there would be no dinner rush, the three of them moved out to the patio beneath the shade of the mossy eucalyptus tree. It wasn't even that hot if you poured a glass of ice water over your head every once in a while. Where were all the customers? Yes, the sky was yellow and gray, yes, the wind smelled of smoke, but so what? The fires couldn't spread to the city.

"People get all panicky," said Lisa, dripping. "It makes them want to squirrel everything away, including their money."

"But if they're going to burn," said Egypt, "shouldn't they spend?"

"Spend spend spend," said Lisa. She held her drink up over her head in punctuation. Half sloshed out.

"What time is Meg cooking again?" asked Ropey.

Egypt's chest dipped. It was just so nice being out on the patio, getting along with but looking better wet than Lisa. She needed to stay here, sitting across from drunk Ropey, who had his eyes on tonight.

"She moved that to tomorrow," Egypt said, "something about a department meeting? I don't know?" Egypt licked the salt from the rim of her drink. Salt? This wasn't a margarita. But Ropey was experimenting, bringing them anything from the bar and Lisa was shouting about how she was going to put all his concoctions on the menu. Egypt hated women who shouted when they got drunk. Her style was to get quiet, slink away, and pose, begging for someone to notice.

15.

At work, Megan buzzed with anticipation. Oh, days like these, with each activity lined up neatly behind the last. She'd finish work, shop for ingredients, then have just the right amount of time to go home and prepare the meal. And so her life would joyously unfold. She was nearly as excited about the shopping and cooking as she was about the meal itself. There was just something about entering your kitchen with a heaping grocery bag in each arm, something about chopping produce in the day's last bit of sun. She'd prep all the produce first, putting each ready ingredient into its own, clean bowl. As she washed and cut, Egypt would perch herself at the kitchen table, chattering away about her problems. Egypt loved a crisis, especially one centered around herself. Lately, she'd been going on and on about a sadness more profound than anything she'd ever experienced. If only Megan could get her to put things into perspective, remind her of the last time she dipped. Keep a journal, see a therapist, she advised Egypt in crisis after crisis, don't you remember feeling desolate for a stretch last year, twice the year before? It's just how it is for all of us. Sometimes life feels really terrible for no apparent reason. So chin up; your pain is not unique.

16.

Lyle unsheathed the dress from its clear plastic bag and tugged at the seam, stretching the bright, new thread into view.

"Great," he said to the seamstress. He counted out seven dollars. "Perfect. Thank you."

"A lovely color," the seamstress said. Lyle swelled like she'd complimented his firstborn. This dress thing was making him vulnerable. He couldn't wait for it to be over, regardless of the outcome. In a way, it seemed a rehearsal for the proposal, which, over the past few weeks, had gained body, transforming from a wispy daydream into a solid, inevitable event in his mind. He was terrified.

As a child, the first real-life proposal Lyle had been aware of was that of an older cousin, surprised by her boyfriend while strolling through a city park. When the newly engaged couple had stopped by a family barbeque the following weekend, Lyle's cousin had been reluctant to recount the details of the proposal and shy when asked to hold out her hand and show off the ring, so, after the couple left, the aunts proclaimed the proposal botched, the ring: a failure. They chuckled about the cousin's fiancé like one would about a very cute puppy who'd peed on himself. This struck a new fear in Lyle's ten-year-old heart. How could a proposal be a failure if the lady said yes? What had the aunts perceived that he had not?

The cousin and the fiancé got married. He became just another husband and then dad standing around with a beer at family events, no longer an object of ridicule. Still, Lyle regarded the fiancé with wonder and fear. Did he know about his shameful mistake? If so, how had he recovered? As a teenager, Lyle had once seen the fiancé at the public library flipping through a book about cleft palates, a condition he and the cousin's second child had been born with years before but immediately cured of, openly crying. Lyle did not approach the man. He'd never before, or after, seen any of his cousins' spouses alone.

Lyle walked the dusty sidewalk back to his Civic with the dress slung over his shoulder. Egypt always went on about how much she wanted to marry him. Multiple times, when drunk, she'd even slumped down to her own knees and proposed.

The October sun was strong despite the layer of smoke yellowing the sky. His shirt dampened beneath his arms and near his belt. Maybe he'd wait to give the dress to her. Feel things out a little more. He could shove it into the back of the closet, where he'd found it a few weeks before. Edendale was quiet. The short stucco houses were sealed up against the heat and the big yard dogs lay on their sides, panting in the barely-shade. In the street, a white sedan crunched over a palm frond, leaving it limp and twitching in the middle of the road.

17.

The grocery store, well-stocked and gleaming, swept Megan off her feet. Though she'd lived in California for nearly three years, the quality of the produce still astounded her every time she shopped. Today, she'd come boldly without a list, with no plan for this dinner besides opening herself to inspiration. Megan wandered the bright, wide aisles feeling very bohemian, fingers hovering above the towers of oranges, grapefruits, and pears. She picked up a bushel of lemongrass, sniffed it, then replaced it. She squeezed a few avocados—perfect as always—but moved on. The tomatoes on the vine, though, stopped her in her tracks. They were exquisite, smelled sun ripened, their dull skins showing no trace of wax. A meal sprang forth from the dark recesses of Megan's mind. She rushed over to the herbs, grabbing two dripping bouquets of parsley and another of mint. Cucumbers, garlic, red onion, chickpeas. There's nothing quite as exhilarating as a basket full of colorful produce. Chicken breasts from the meat wall, pitas in aisle six. At the cheese fridge, Megan chose a supple feta still swimming in its brine.

Of course, she'd gather lemons in the yard.

The kitchen was not as sunny as Megan had wanted it to be, and when she'd arrived home with her grocery bags, neither Egypt nor Ropey, whose lunch shifts should have ended hours ago, were there. Instead it was just her and the cat, who meowed desperately at the door.

"There are coyotes out there," Megan said. "They want to eat you."

She unpacked the produce, washed it, and began to chop. The herbs stuck to her fingers. Everything was too wet. Her hair fell in front of her face and she pushed it back with the heel of her hand so as not to get the sticking herb bits all over her head. They got everywhere anyways. Megan put the knife down. Stepped back and counted to ten. Told herself she was improving things. As her life moved forward, she made it better. She could teach. She could make a meal for her friends.

Still, she'd like to empty out the kitchen cupboards and give them a good scrub-down. She'd like to stick some contact paper to the shelves before she loaded all their chipped mugs, mismatched plates, and half-eaten boxes of instant rice back in. Once, she'd purchased a set of matching tins in various sizes in which they could collectively store all their dry goods. She'd put her own in the tins, but everyone else's were still in the cupboards, fluffing white flour dust all over the shelves that she wanted to clean.

Tomatoes, parsley, cucumber, mint. She chopped it all. No one came home. The daylight was fading, but she didn't want to turn on the kitchen light. Turning on the kitchen light would be an admission. She pushed hateful accusations out of her head, thought about how she could put in a vegetable garden out back—one of those raised beds made of railroad ties. She wanted to paint the front door bright red and do something about the dead grass and dust in the front yard. People all over LA were putting in drought-friendly landscaping. She could make a pleasant arrangement out of rocks and cacti, too, if she had a little help. She wanted to live somewhere with air conditioning. She wanted to live somewhere with clean counters and fresh breezes stirring her floral dresses. Her hair fell in her face again. She pushed it away, this time getting all sorts of herbs stuck into her hairline. She hadn't pulled her hair back because she didn't want to dent her curl. Megan cursed her vanity. Stepped back and counted to ten again. She sliced the chicken and then put it in a baggie with some garlic, oil, and lemon juice. Finally, the front latch clicked.

"Hello?" Lyle, home first. He sat at the table, oblivious of the fact that it was going all wrong. The collar of his work shirt was ringed yellow though she knew he cleaned it often. He needed new clothes but did not buy them because he was supporting Egypt. Egypt, who wasn't here. She imagined Egypt and Ropey, doing it in some thorny bramble. Him behind, her bent forward, stupid tiny breasts swinging with each of his thrusts. She'd be up on her tiptoes. Smoky sky, coyotes howling. Damn Egypt for treating Lyle the way she did.

Megan waited as long as she could bear before she took the chicken out of the marinade, skewered it, and cooked it on their panini press. She put the kebabs in foil to keep them warm. She mixed the yogurt sauce. Lyle checked his watch.

"When do Egypt and Ropey usually get home?" he asked.

"Any minute now," said Megan. "Hey, the stains are getting better." She gestured toward a corner of the wall where Captain America's bloodstains were exactly the same. At the beginning of the month, they'd spent hours together on hands and knees scrubbing. It had been nice! If she had to build a home from the twisted wing of an aircraft with anyone, she'd want it to be Lyle.

"That they are," said Lyle.

When it was too dark to keep pretending, she switched on the light above the kitchen table. The orb glowed, dead flies speckling the bottom curve of the opaque glass. They sat there in its small spotlight, waiting. He must know, she thought, thinking again of Egypt's small, swinging breasts. They tried calling each a few times.

"We should probably just eat," Megan said.

"I'll wait."

A car passed, its headlights sweeping over them and the wall.

"They're probably together, right?" said Lyle.

Megan didn't know what to say. Of course they were.

"I'll try Ropey again," Lyle said. He looked at his phone, which sat on the table directly in front of him but didn't reach for it. "I picked up the dress today."

Megan nodded. Most of Egypt's belongings were things Megan had discarded. She wondered if Lyle noticed, or if all her old dresses, flats, cheap jewelry, and bags morphed for him once Egypt pulled them on. Egypt was skinny. Her skin was translucent and papery and her joints were too big. Megan considered herself more objectively attractive than Egypt, but the world was filled with men who liked women with bodies like children's and Megan's shoulders and quads were hardened from years of discipline.

Megan made Lyle a plate.

"You're becoming a really amazing cook," he said after his first bite.

"Thanks. I was thinking I might sign up for a cooking class." She hadn't been, but now, watching Lyle's smile of approval, she decided she would. Maybe he'd join her. Captain America hopped up on the table. His face seemed narrower, more angular. Megan fed him a spoonful of tabbouleh.

"I'm worried," said Lyle.

"About their safety?"

"Yeah."

"I wouldn't be." Megan pulled the cat onto her lap, spreading the thinning hair on his back to get a better look at his spine. Had it always been this pronounced? She'd bug Ropey about the treatment again, just as soon as she could catch him in the right mood.

Megan and Lyle ate very slowly, turning toward the door at every outdoor sound. After it was no longer possible to draw out the meal, Lyle took their plates to the sink. He washed, she dried. The cat paced behind them. Dishes finished, kitchen spotless besides the foil-covered plates waiting on the counter for Egypt and Ropey, they sat back down at the table. Finally, there were footsteps on the front stairs. The front door opened.

Edendale

"Why are you guys hanging out in the dark?" Ropey called. The living room lights flicked on. The two of them came into the kitchen, Egypt hanging on Ropey's arm. Ropey scanned the kitchen, looked from Megan to Lyle.

"You said Meg cancelled dinner." He shook Egypt off. "She told me you cancelled dinner."

"Yeah," Egypt said. "That's what I thought."

Megan looked from Egypt to Ropey, feeling sick. "Why would you think that?"

"Because that's what you told me."

"When?"

"Yesterday."

"I didn't even see you yesterday."

"Egypt came in at the end of my shift," said Ropey. "She told me that you had a meeting." He was drunk. "Meg, I feel like an asshole. I'm so sorry. It smells amazing in here."

Captain America leapt off the table and ran into the dark of the living room.

"I swear he sees ghosts," said Lyle.

Megan was not going to let Lyle change the subject. Egypt had to be held accountable for at least one thing.

"So you asked Ropey to stay out and get drunk after your shifts because you thought I told you dinner was postponed."

"Yeah."

"So where were we when I told you this yesterday?"

"That's enough," said Lyle. "They made a mistake."

"I'm just curious where this memory came from?" Megan said. "Are you okay, Egypt? Are you hallucinating now?"

"Meg. That's enough." Lyle took Egypt by the arm and led her upstairs.

I am on your side! Megan wanted to call after him.

18.

Egypt followed Lyle upstairs, feeling Ropey's eyes hot on her back as she climbed. She'd forgotten that her lie was a lie until she'd seen Lyle and Megan at the empty table, waiting. Why wait? She'd never asked them to wait for her. At the top of the stairs, Egypt turned to rescue her evening with Ropey with a co-conspiratorial glance, but he wasn't there. She went stiff with shock. He hadn't watched her climb. To combat her disappointment, she took Lyle by the wrist and led him down the hall to their bedroom, deciding to be very loud in bed.

They entered their room. On the bed: her yellow dress, smooth and flat. It didn't look like something that belonged on a body.

"Oh," said Egypt, dropping Lyle's wrist.

"I know that fixing the dress doesn't fix that day," Lyle said, "but I want you to know that it will never happen again. When you're in trouble, I come. Period." His upper lip was dotted with sweat and he spoke too softly. He was always speaking too softly. It made her murderous when she couldn't hear what he said.

"Okay," said Egypt. "Thank you."

"You like it? You're not upset?" He lifted the dress into the air by the straps and swung it side to side. The phantom woman danced. The dress looked different. Cheaper, shiny, like something you'd buy folded in a plastic bag from a costume store. Egypt wished reality would just stay one way. Meanwhile, Megan and Ropey's voices floated up the stairs, all garbled. She couldn't make out their conversation, and this pissed her off extraordinarily. Like, were they talking about her?

19.

Before Captain America lived with Ropey, he lived with a woman named Jennie in a cottage a few blocks from the ocean. Jennie grew vegetables instead of grass on their patch of front yard. One year, the garden produced more cucumbers than Jennie had intended, so they spent their August weekends packing the little monsters into jars with vinegar, garlic, and dill. Captain America enjoyed these weekends. He liked when the breeze swooped in, blowing the garlic skins off the counter and into the dusty corners of the kitchen floor, and he liked to steal sprigs of dill whenever Jennie turned her back. The dill sprigs were both tasty and easy to carry around. Best, he liked that pickling made Jennie tired. She'd lie on their bed or their couch afterwards, letting Captain America walk across her belly and chest as many times as he wanted before he settled down. Captain America's name was not Captain America when he lived with Jennie. It was a different word, something she didn't have to open her mouth as many times to say. After Jennie sliced her arms open with a razor and bled into their bed until she died, Captain America lived outside for a while. Outside, there were songbirds, small rodents, and many other cats. After that, he came to live with Ropey, who brought him to share many different houses and apartments with a wide assortment of people. Of all these people, Captain America liked Megan the best because she was a lot like Jennie in both scent and habit. Megan, like Jennie, insisted on keeping him inside.

20.

On the news alongside the fire coverage: a home out in the Simi Valley had become infested with dozens of snakes seeking a new den after theirs had been destroyed. The family listened to the snakes moving through their walls for three nights, finding one coiled in a kitchen drawer and another stretched behind the couch skirt, before fleeing.

21.

Ropey lay flat in the center of his bed with his hands stretched out by his sides, third eye activated. He'd been meditating in the dark before Egypt had pulled his tapestry aside, flooding his room with sunlight from the kitchen. They were the only ones at home.

"Do you remember, last month, that woman by the lake?" Egypt stepped into his room, letting the tapestry go behind her. Shadows danced as it swung back and forth across the bright doorway. Egypt loomed at the foot of his bed. She seemed capable of swallowing him whole.

"Of course I remember that."

"And you remember my dress?" Egypt began to pace. "How she ripped it?" Around his bed to the window, then, turning, all the way around the opposite side again. Ropey thought about all the effort he was putting into being open with her, wondering how good openness could possibly be if it was born of effort instead of love. He believed it impossible to feel anything but love for a person if you saw them and felt he was inches from getting his eyes around Egypt. He kept his palms open, hoping she would and wouldn't climb into his bed.

The room darkened as the tapestry settled.

"I haven't been able to go back there," said Egypt.

Egypt knew she was pacing in that she understood that Ropey saw her pacing but couldn't quite comprehend her body's movement with her own, solitary mind. Instead, she imagined what it would feel like to be him, what it would be like to stare up at herself. How did she look to him? She hoped, with all her might, that he found her attractive. What does it mean if the person who sees you doesn't want you? Round and round his bed. If only he'd jump up, grab her by her shoulders, and command her to stop. If she were him, she'd drag herself down into the bed.

"So you remember it, my yellow sundress?" she said again.

"Sure," he lied. He remembered the event, the distress, but not quite the article of clothing.

"Lyle got it fixed for me. Isn't that nice?"

Ropey was glad his headboard was flush to the window, or she'd be circling him like a shark. She gained momentum with each turn. She seemed eleven feet tall and strong enough to plow through him, splintering wood, tearing batting from springs, and severing his chest from his neck.

"I look great in that yellow sundress," she said. "I'm not ashamed to say it. People want you to be ashamed. They'd like me to pretend I haven't noticed how I get noticed. But that would make me a liar. Isn't that worse? You're allowed to know that you're smart or kind or athletic or whatever, but you're not supposed to notice that people want to fuck you. I'm not saying that I'm something special. Just that I'm twenty-three and thin and female with okay skin. That's just how it goes."

Ropey considered this. He dug up, maybe fabricated, a blurry memory of how she looked in yellow. Gaudy, bright: the hard color would make her freckled skin seem gray. On the day when the woman ripped Egypt's yellow dress, he'd brought home a pizza from Little Wink. *I'm so lonely,* she'd said when he found her alone in the backyard—Megan was in the kitchen breading fish—so he'd offered her a slice then went inside to get her favorite blue nail polish. And yes, of course he wanted to fuck her, but he couldn't understand why she thought that was such a special thing.

"Well," said Ropey. "That's nice of Lyle to get it fixed for you, then."

"It is," said Egypt. "I think it's the nicest thing."

Edendale

"He's a great guy."

"You're right. I don't deserve him."

Captain America jumped from the windowsill and ran out of the room, sending a shiver up the tapestry as he crossed beneath it.

"I have this wart on my finger," Egypt said. "All I need to do is go to the doctor and they'll freeze it off. And if it doesn't work the first time, I could go back again and again until it did. But I don't. I can't."

"A lot of people don't like going to the doctor."

"No," she said. "It's like, why didn't I even think of fixing the dress myself?"

"You've got a lot on your mind."

Egypt shook her head without slowing her pace. He wasn't listening to her. How could she make him understand? She felt that if he didn't understand, no one ever would. She tried again.

"It's like with Megan. Have you ever looked through Megan's clothes? She knows how to keep a wardrobe. My clothes, I had that dress and it was so nice for a while, I thought I'd figured out how to have clothes that are nice. I'm always starting. Do you feel like you're always starting?"

"Yes," said Ropey, though he wasn't quite sure what she was asking him to understand. Keep talking, he thought. Get it out. He felt like a guru; a tiny, helpful god. He looked toward his dresser. No money had gone missing for a while, now. He shuddered at the small possibility that he'd been mistaken. But, Jesus, she was still talking.

"Once I brought lice into one of our sublets," said Egypt. "I didn't know, and then when I finally did know, I realized I'd known all along. I'd been seeing them everywhere—in my brush, on my headrest, in the shower—but not really processing it. And then one night Meg said that I'd been scratching like a maniac for a few weeks and then looked in my head. As soon as she told me, even before she looked, all these moments when I'd seen the lice but had my mind on other things came rushing back."

"Lice?" Ropey's scalp began to itch.

"They were huge and black. I must've had them for a month for them to grow that big. And there I was, going about my normal life. I'd even bought a bottle of Head & Shoulders because my scalp was itchy. Whenever I held my hand out in the shower to rinse it off, the foam crawled. But even then, with a handful of bugs, I didn't realize. Another person would have known sooner. I'm not capable of taking care of things."

Egypt stopped walking. She covered her face with her hands.

"Hey," said Ropey. Maybe he preferred the pacing after all. "I'm right here."

"But who are you?"

"Jon Ropes. Your roommate. Your friend."

"Why?"

"Because I am," said Ropey.

"I'm not talking about lice," said Egypt.

"Then tell me what you're talking about."

"I've been very sad."

It was Ropey's turn to ask why.

"Well," said Egypt, "I think it's because I'm all alone."

There it was. He was sure he saw. If this was all, it could be solved with contemplation and time. Ropey felt very wise.

"Why is that a sad thing?" he asked.

"So you agree?" asked Egypt. "You think I'm alone?"

In his dark bedroom, Ropey moved aside, beckoning her into bed with him. He held her head against his chest, smelling the grease in her hair. When Egypt was new at Little Wink and working her mysterious, out-of-town boyfriend into every conversation, Ropey had assumed that Lyle was either a fabrication or an exaggeration, summoned to ward off his light-hearted advances. Then Lyle had arrived in the flesh and Ropey, seeing the wide-eyed way she stared at him, understood Egypt as a woman obsessed.

Egypt readjusted, making sure that Ropey could feel her pubic bone on the side of his thigh, imagining being him, imagining the feel of her own pubic bone. She made sure that both their shirts lifted slightly. Torso skin touched torso skin. So maybe there was such a thing as connection, the layers falling away. So maybe she wasn't alone.

She pretended to fall asleep, and while pretending to fall asleep she actually fell asleep. When she woke, Ropey had left—he worked the late afternoon shift on Thursdays—and Captain America stretched out on the pillow, framing her head like a mangy crown.

22.

"Pack comfortable, athletic clothes, a bathing suit, and something warm to sleep in," said Lyle. "I'll take care of everything else."

"Shoes?" asked Egypt.

"Tennis shoes and flip flops!"

23.

They left the city early, while the light on the concrete was still pastel. Egypt, curled in the passenger's seat, felt oddly tranquil. Maybe it was the leaving, maybe she was cured, or maybe there was just a quota of violent discontent a body would allow itself before the calm set in, despite circumstances unchanged. The freeways were empty. As Lyle curved them through interchanges, underpasses and overpasses whishing by, Egypt toyed with the idea that he'd been right: all they'd needed was a trip. She thought of Ropey, who she didn't love, but who perhaps maybe someday she could love more deeply than she loved Lyle if given the chance. Without the usual press of traffic, the freeway looked clean, sun-bleached.

They drove north through farmland on a two-lane highway. Spiny irrigation systems arched over the dry crops.

Egypt eased even further into the journey. Her legs did not twitch. Maybe it was the lack of responsibility.

Edendale

Today, any discomfort or harm that might befall her would be Lyle's fault. The idea was freeing.

He squeezed her knee. They cut back out toward the coast. When she saw the bluff and the empty beach below, a little defeated voice inside her said *oh*. She understood. She looked down at her nails, regretting that they were short and unpainted.

"Okay," said Lyle when he was finished unpacking the car.

"Okay," Egypt said in response. She followed him down the bluff to the beach, where she lay on a blanket drinking white wine as he pitched the tent and gathered driftwood for a fire. Though it couldn't have been past three, he built the fire and began to cook, using a pocketknife to slice an orange block of cheddar onto a paper plate balanced on his knee. He'd brought a frying pan, a shrink-wrapped package of boneless chicken thighs, and tortillas. As the chicken sizzled, another group set up camp about a mile down the beach. In the opposite direction, a woman threw a tennis ball into the surf for two yellow dogs. There was a moment of high stakes: the chicken needed to come out of the pan before it burned, but Lyle couldn't find another plate. Egypt watched, finding his panic endearing. At the last moment, the chicken went on top of the cheese, the tortillas went into the pan, and then the whole melted mess went into the tortillas in one blob. The quesadillas were soft, greasy, delicious.

"This place is supposed to be a butterfly refuge," he said as they ate. They'd seen no butterflies. His distress radiated.

"It's beautiful anyways," Egypt said. She liked this dynamic: her comforting him. "I think butterflies would have actually been a little over the top."

"Really?" said Lyle, hopeful, vulnerable. Had he always had those dimples? "The website said that monarchs stopped here every year during their migration."

One of the yellow dogs cantered over to the fire and asked Lyle for some of his quesadilla. Lyle flipped him the entire thing. The owner ran up, apologetic, with the other yellow dog trailing behind her. She was gray-haired and athletic. Her breezy shirt-pants combo was subdued but obviously expensive, which made Egypt trust her immensely. While Lyle assured the woman that her dog was no bother at all, Egypt fantasized about confiding in her.

"Lyle's about to propose to me!" she'd say, as they rushed arm in arm away from the fire.

"Wow," the woman would respond, "how do you feel about that?"

"Does a person know how they feel about anything? Are you telling me you actually know how you feel about things?"

Edendale

"Sure I do. See my gray hair?"

"Well, I feel a few contradictory things all at once," Egypt would explain. "Like, it seems like a good idea to marry the kind of guy that gives his entire quesadilla to a dog on the beach, especially if that guy is Lyle, but also, I've been very sad lately and I think it's partially his fault. For example, he paid for our bed, which makes me feel like a concubine, and then, when a woman stripped naked in the park and tore my yellow sundress, he didn't know to come. Mostly, I love him, but love isn't what I expected. The layers didn't fall away. We're separate. There are still places in me he cannot see. And vice versa."

"So?"

"I just, I thought, if it were real love, well, wouldn't we share, like, a soul?"

"Real love?" the woman would say, "Souls? Are you upset about the disappearance of your tooth fairy, too?"

"No! No!" Egypt would respond. "I misspoke. I meant to say core, not soul. Essence-ness. Personality. Whatever you call the deepest, mortal thing."

"Tomayto, tomahto," the woman would tell Egypt. "It's fine. Just go live your life. You'll do some insignificant stuff, you'll marry someone or you won't—it won't matter to anyone, not even you—and then you'll die. Now, look at my dogs. They're purebred.

If they had a litter, I could sell the puppies for five thousand dollars each."

Okay, Egypt thought. *Okay okay okay.* The woman and her dogs trotted off unaware of this exchange as Egypt nibbled at her quesadilla in contemplative silence. Once the trio became specks playing fetch in the far surf again, Egypt offered Lyle half of her remaining meal. He refused, so she gobbled it all up and licked the grease off her fingers. The sun began its descent. Lyle wiped his hands on his shorts and suggested a walk up on the bluffs. Egypt agreed, smoothing her hair. On the bluffs, when she noticed him fumbling in his pocket, Egypt turned to the ocean to give him some privacy. The woman and her dogs were gone, the waves, disappointing. They crashed into the curved coastline at odd angles, unable to settle into a soothing rhythm. The seabirds were nice, though. They sounded how you'd expect.

"Egypt," said Lyle, so she took a deep breath in and turned to find him down on one knee. She struggled to focus on his weird little speech. She was very much in her own body. How strange, living in a moment that you'd always known would come. This must be what it feels like to finally die. She tried to describe it to herself in words so she could remember it, but couldn't tell if reality was suspended or if she'd never felt anything so

Edendale

real before. She felt solid. Like a rod in the middle of a lightning field.

She said "of course" instead of "yes" because she'd always planned to—she thought it sounded more passionate—ever since she was a little girl.

Afterwards, they wandered around on the bluffs for a while, ducking around low-branched live oaks, the thorny brush grabbing at their socks, before heading back down to the beach. Lyle unpacked a bottle of champagne, a pre-rolled joint, and then a flask of whisky. They had sex twice: once in the sand and once in the tent. In between, Egypt curled into a ball and wept about the death of her mother, six years before. What happened was that she'd somehow forgotten and, while Lyle was jerking around inside her, was struck by the sudden impulse to call and tell her about the engagement followed by the sudden realization that she was dead, which ripped her grief wide open again. They went to sleep with their sleeping bags zipped together. Sometime in the night, Egypt woke to Lyle hovering above her on all fours.

"Sorry," he said, "The wind's coming from your side. I didn't want you to get cold."

But, even with him transferred to the wind side, she did get cold, waking often, and when they emerged in the morning into the already high sun, she was shocked to discover that the bottoms of their feet were black from tar that they hadn't known lay hidden in the sand.

November

1.

When Lisa called to fire her, Egypt was eating spoonfuls of jam from a jar in the fridge.

"I hate to do this over the phone," Lisa said, "I just don't want to waste your time, making you come in and all."

Phone to her ear, Egypt watched the wind tear through their backyard. It was November and the Santa Anas careened down from the mountains, bringing that hot, fast, flammable air. The dry branches of the lemon tree swayed and rattled. Dead leaves tumbleweeded across the patio. One particularly strong gust had overturned the lounge chairs, throwing them against the tilting fence. Now, their broken rubber bands slapped against their metal frames.

"Can I at least stay on the roster?" Egypt asked. "No shifts, but, you know, in case someone needs a cover?"

"Um, I guess that's fine," said Lisa, and Egypt knew it was a lie. She thought of Ropey at the bar within earshot, and how, if the wind blew any harder, all the sleek houses with their shelf decks would come tumbling down the hill. She reminded herself that the day job was never the objective. Still, her lungs felt encased in lead.

"I'll see you around," said Lisa. "Don't be a stranger, okay?"

"Sure. Thanks."

Egypt put down her phone. With the windows closed, the kitchen stunk. Like bong water and old fruit. Captain America appeared behind her and gurgled in sympathy.

"It doesn't matter," she told him. The ring rubbed up against her wart, which was uncomfortable but prevented it from slipping off her finger. She thought that this could maybe be interpreted as a favorable sign. "I have a new perspective," she said to the cat as she held back tears, "so it's just an inconvenience, really."

To prove her point, Egypt turned on the front burner of the stove and cheerfully plucked a stick of incense from the jar on the windowsill, lighting it in the quivering blue flame. She turned to pop the lit stick into the ceramic frog's little mouth hole, but, as she turned, she knocked her elbow on the countertop. Pain radiated up into her shoulder and down into her fingers, the force of the impact simultaneously vibrating up the stick and causing its lit end to crumble. The flame fell, landing on Egypt's foot. She kicked. The loose ash spread across the linoleum in a fan, leaving a single red ember stuck into the top of her foot. Egypt bent to flick it off but discovered that the ember had burned its way down a few layers, lodging itself in her skin. She picked around a little. It was really in there.

When the pain came, it came strong, searing past flesh and into bone. Egypt staggered. She grabbed onto the countertop for support and then lifted her foot into the sink. The smell of her skin, singed, wafted up. She ran the faucet. Needles shuddered up her leg into her stomach as the cold water hit the burn.

The cat gurgled again. Her job, lost. Herself, engaged.

"Look what you made me do," Egypt said. Captain America hissed back, his lips receding away from needle teeth. Egypt had never heard Captain America hiss before. It was much more convincing than she'd imagined it could be.

"Are you a snake?" Egypt joked to mask her fear. The burn pulsed beneath the water. She thought she might vomit or scream. The cat dashed back behind Ropey's tapestry. "Just kidding!" Egypt called after him, but she'd managed to horrify herself with the thought. Now, she could practically see his four legs retreating back up into his body, his tail widening until it matched his blackening torso in girth. Maybe that was the explanation for the sores covering his thinning body. Maybe their cat was molting. Transformed into a snake, Captain America would slide coolly over Ropey's dark floor, waiting in a coil under the bed.

2.

There would be no outdoor recess at Megan's school. This dry wind was too dangerous. It kicked up debris, adding dirt and plant particles to the already bad air. A tree or a branch or anything really could be blown loose and fall on the playground. The kids had to stay inside.

On the news: forced blackouts in high-risk areas. The mustard-tangled hills were dried tinder, and lines downed by wind would spark new fires if live. This, of course, was outside Los Angeles. Even hilly Edendale was too dense, too built up, for there to be any real risk at home. And there was rain in the forecast for tomorrow. Relief was in sight.

"Let's play wind!" said Megan to the group. "Whoosh, you are wind! How do you move your arms, wind? What do you do with your mouth?"

The children twirled and flapped. They puffed out their cheeks and blew. Some giggled, many coughed. Though these were children of careful parents, of air purifiers and indoor playground memberships, in Los Angeles the wild autumn air always finds its way in.

Back home, Megan parked out front and rushed in to find the hot dust twirling through her living room. The kitchen slider was wide open. Megan's body clenched in worry. The cat. Where was the cat?

Egypt slept beneath the lemon tree on a ratty beach towel placed directly on the ground. Dirt whipped over her face.

"Egypt?" Megan nudged Egypt's side with the toe of her sneaker. There was validation in catching Egypt in the act, a sly kind of happiness in meeting what she'd expected all along. The happiness lingered, inappropriate and unwelcome, lacing itself into the dread now spreading through Megan's body. Where was Captain America? The rotting lemon stink mixed with the dust and leaf bits in the air. Megan pulled her shirt up over her nose. "Hey," she said. "Was Captain America out here with you?

Egypt's eyes fluttered but remained closed. Megan nudged her with her shoe again.

"Egypt, where is the cat?"

She nudged her harder. Egypt propped herself up on her elbows. She wiped the dried spit from her mouth with the back of her hand.

Edendale

"The cat?"

"We're not letting him out," said Megan. "Was he out here with you?"

"Um, I think so."

Megan's stomach flipped. She went back into the kitchen, calling for the cat as she opened a can of seafood feast. He neither appeared at the crack of the can, nor when she tapped the spoon against his porcelain bowl.

Egypt came in from outside, still bleary-eyed. "I'm sure he's fine," she said.

"How?"

"He knows his way home."

Megan emptied the seafood feast into Captain America's porcelain bowl. He did not come. Looking hopefully towards Ropey's tapestry, Megan tapped the bowl with the spoon again, but there was no characteristic shudder, no Captain America trotting out from beneath with his tail curled upward in happy anticipation of his meal.

"He's an animal," Egypt said. "He can take care of himself."

Megan closed her eyes and counted to ten, commanding her body to relax, her mind to drift. To do this, she summoned the slack bodies of her students during nap time. Even with the branches of the playground trees slamming against the windows, she'd been able to make them feel safe enough for sleep. Megan began to feel the calm of a job well done wash over her, loosening her set jaw and fists. Then, suddenly, she remembered how, after nap time, Lucas had tapped her on the shoulder and asked if she could please close the windows (they were, of course, already closed), saying that under his skin was itchy with all of the dust. She'd understood his statement so deeply that it shifted something in her gut, but she'd been in the middle of helping Stella with her zipper, and after that Jasper had spilled her paint water, and, by the time she was free, had forgotten Lucas's distress. Megan opened her eyes and walked a wide circle around Egypt to put the wet food bowl on Captain America's mat. She was failing, failing. She grabbed the cat's favorite bag of treats and went out into the street, calling his name. The street was abandoned; everyone had shuttered themselves inside against the bad air. Megan walked the neighborhood, shaking the bag of treats. Trash blustered around the gravel shoulder. Everyone's dead gardens rattled. You can only give a person so much leeway. Still, this was Egypt. Bird-boned, with skin like paper and wrists so small you were tempted to break them. Shaking the bag of treats up and down the street, Megan found her reservoir was not yet depleted.

3.

During the summer between their first and second years of college, Megan took a few days off her babysitting job to visit Egypt who, with no real home to return to, was spending break at a relative's cottage on the Georgia coast. Though the plane tickets cost nearly a quarter of her summer earnings, all of which she needed badly to get through the coming year of social obligations at school, the trip seemed necessary. College had been a revelation. Home felt like exile.

The cottage was not a cottage, but a sprawling beachfront home with a series of outbuildings and a saltwater pool. Megan thought that maybe it was a mansion, but since there were no curved staircases or golden chandeliers she wasn't quite sure how to file it. Instead, there were plush, recklessly white couches, blinds made of solid wood instead of plastic, framed pictures of freckled relatives smiling from the decks of teak boats, and a double-wide fridge paneled over to blend into the kitchen cabinetry. The cottage seemed to belong to no one and everyone. Egypt's relatives breezed in and out, each unpacking another bag of groceries so that the counters were cluttered with baguettes, boxes of nutty crackers, and bottles of wine, and the fridge brimmed full of butcher-marinated meats and blocks of veined, crumbling cheeses. There were no men of working age among these guests, just sandy-colored, make-up free women in loose, neutral clothing, plus their children and au pairs, and no one seemed to care that Megan and Egypt were eating for free. During the day, they lay by the pool or the ocean snacking from cheese plates prepared by various cousins and aunts. At night they sat around the fire pit drinking wine from deep, fragile glasses. Megan struggled to keep track of who was who. Everyone was thin and symmetrical and had a name that seemed meant for something else. Among the older women there was a Bradley, a Warren, a Poppy. A set of school-aged twins were named Poet and Elixir.

Back in New Hampshire, Megan's house, which she would from now on refer to as her parents' house, seemed to be made of vinyl and toothpicks. She recoiled from the thin bath towels, the magnet-covered fridge, and the cupboard stocked with Ritz crackers, Hamburger Helper, and powders for making iced tea.

Edendale

Megan spent the remainder of the summer dreaming of quality, of substance. Her mother's careful eye shadow devastated her.

4.

The boys came home. First Ropey, then Lyle. Megan told them each what had happened. Though she contorted her sentences to avoid making implications, both understood it was Egypt's fault. How else? Who else?

"He wouldn't have gone far," said Lyle. "It's hellish out there."

The branches of the lemon tree banged up against the kitchen window. Megan tried and failed to run her fingers through her wind-tangled hair.

"Here's what we're going to do," she said. She instructed her roommates to gather all the objects they thought might lure Captain America out and divided Edendale into four not-quite-equal quadrants, assigning them based on what she estimated her roommates' cat hunting abilities to be. The group stepped out onto the porch.

Edendale

"We'll find him," said Lyle, tying a handkerchief around his nose and mouth against the dust-filled air. He offered another handkerchief to Egypt, who refused.

"Or he'll come back on his own," said Ropey, shaking a jingly catnip mouse.

"He's going to hide," said Megan. "This wind."

Ropey, forearms still sticky with soda and alcohol from work, walked through his hilly quadrant with his hand over his eyes, shielding himself from dirt kicked up and whipped around. When he'd first found Captain America, there'd been splinters stuck in the soft pads of the cat's paws. He'd removed them with tweezers, then used rubbing alcohol to clean the wounds.

"Come on out, little dude," he shouted. "We love you, let's go home." As he said this, he felt a pang of guilt. If the cat wanted to live with them, he would. Ropey wasn't looking to keep anyone prisoner. Still, he could walk around in the dark if that's what Megan needed.

The rubbing alcohol, had, of course, made the cat yelp and squirm, but the wounds healed without infection. Today, when he came home and saw the grief on Megan's face, his first thought had been that Egypt killed herself upon being fired. Now, he imagined how she'd do it, arranging herself on the bathroom floor in a cinematic pose, bottle of pills rolled dramatically from her limp hand. But no, Egypt would never kill herself because being dead would mean she wouldn't be around to get off on Lyle's reaction to her death. Ropey imagined a suicide note but no body found, Egypt watching Lyle from behind a wig and dark glasses as he mourned. You're not doing it right, she'd say eventually, a ghost stepping out from the crowd. Your grief doesn't match my fantasy.

Lyle used a stick to sweep around in the dry roadside brush, whistling "You Are My Sunshine," because, sometimes, Captain America liked when he whistled.

Egypt lagged behind. He thought she should be searching with more energy—this was her fault after all—but said nothing because he didn't want to start a fight. Also, he felt capable of bringing more than enough energy for the both of them. Fill in her gaps, compensate for her flaws. This was practice for marriage, right? They wouldn't be evaluated as individuals anymore, but as a team. A good husband picks up what his wife drops (though, wondered Lyle, what had his mother ever dropped? With her coupons and her clean nails, Lyle's mother was perfect). Lyle liked to pick up. Lyle liked to put together. Lyle liked Egypt, who'd absentmindedly lost Ropey's cat.

Edendale

"Come on out, big guy," Lyle said, making his voice low and gentle. "We got you. You're safe." Egypt stood in the center of the road, looking at the sky. "Cars can't see you there," he said to her. "Come over here."

She walked to him on the gravelly shoulder. A strong gust brought in a metallic campfire smell.

"If I got hit by a car," she said, "it'd be payday."

"I think we can find a better way to make rent."

"Aren't you mad at me?" asked Egypt.

"For what?"

"The cat."

"Accidents happen."

"What if I told you I did it on purpose?"

Lyle laughed, a little unsure. A helicopter padded overhead, heading northeast. Large and double-bladed: not news, but water. Beyond the dark hills, Lyle made out a muted glow. His body registered fire. When had this one broken out?

Egypt laughed, too. "I didn't, but it kind of feels like I did. You know?"

"I do," said Lyle, feeling very close to her. "Guilt is an awful thing." This would be his life, conversations like these with this very pretty, very sensitive woman. He couldn't believe his luck.

* * *

Megan lingered behind. Once her roommates were all out of sight, she dipped back into the house. Inside, she scraped Captain America's wet food into the trash, dumped his dry food back into the bag, and poured his water down the sink. Megan washed all three of the bowls, wiped them dry, and hid them beneath the kitchen sink. Emptied of his things, the corner looked strange to her, like a face without a nose, but she told herself she was right to put the bowls away immediately. If she'd waited any longer, getting rid of them would have been as impossible as removing a gravestone.

Back outside, Megan went door-to-door, showing anyone who answered pictures of Captain America on her phone.

"Take my number," she told each of them. "Just in case."

As she walked, the dust-laden air started to smell of smoke. Megan coughed, pulling her shirt up over her face and nose. Her eyes watered. She checked the LAFD's Twitter. A brush fire had broken out in a ravine park just across the freeway. Her pulse thumped against her skull. She told herself it would be okay. There was rain in the forecast for tomorrow.

Sirens wailed. Helicopters beat toward the scene. They'd put it out in a matter of hours, and soon there would be rain. Megan opened a can of seafood feast.

Edendale

She thought of her students, her roommates, their orange tabby cat. All the vulnerable creatures of the world who needed her attention. It made her want to lie down on the asphalt and weep. She felt she could not do enough. As soon as she got one sector of her world figured out, another collapsed. She didn't have enough good in her to be good to everyone. There was never enough time, never enough energy in her hard, imperfect body to do all she wanted for everyone who needed it. But if she didn't find Captain America, no one would. She didn't believe that Ropey was actually looking—he was probably just ambling along, mentally writing some lazy manifesto about the cat's right to choose to get eaten alive by a lucky coyote. And Lyle, normally helpful, had recently been useless in his post-engagement haze. Egypt would not find the cat, unless she did, and if she did she would be praised out of proportion for surpassing everyone's estimate of her worth.

Egypt left Lyle on the dark hill, claiming she thought she'd be more effective searching on her own, telling herself she was about to go search on her own, while also knowing that she was seeking out Ropey. She found him in the bright glass box of the 7-Eleven and waited outside in the dark, balancing on a cement parking block as she watched him stack sardine cans and carry them to the register. Through the glass, Egypt watched him pay, shove his wallet back into his jeans, and smile at a teenage couple as he turned his body to pass between them and a sunglass display on his way to the door.

She called to him. He didn't hear her.

The teenagers left the 7-Eleven, walking between Egypt and Ropey on their way to the crosswalk. Egypt hated the girl, her tan, muscular legs, the little shorts she wore for her boyfriend.

She called to him again.

"Oh, hi," Ropey said.

"I had to find you," said Egypt, "Do you hate me?"

A helicopter passed overhead.

"Is there another one?" Ropey asked.

Egypt shrugged. The dry, dirty wind clawed at the exposed skin of her face and arms. "Do you hate me?" she asked again.

"I don't hate you," Ropey said, but the way he winced as he turned away told her otherwise.

Even with his ears flattened to his head, Captain America picked up the crinkle of his treat bag. He smelled home. He smelled Megan. He smelled his seafood feast. The muscles in his legs twitched. He would like to run to her, but he knew that he couldn't. He was small and in unknown territory. There'd been some fun birds, a wily lizard. But then he'd found himself in this thicket, where every leaf and twig and bramble smelled of predator. His instincts told him that to stir was to attract dangerous attention. He must be still, silent.

"Captain America!" He smelled Lyle. His treat bag shook. The wind blew hot dust into his eyes. He squeezed them shut, further camouflaging himself. He'd hide here until the world smelled safe again.

"I'm going to check the park," Ropey said. He felt like a villain; he hadn't been planning to go there before Egypt had cornered him. She looked up at him, head back, neck exposed, eyes wide and wet. He found her transparency terrifying—each gesture pathetic, pleading, electric—and enjoyed the feeling of her cold awful hand on his wrist. He let her follow him.

The wind came in gusts, kicking up trash and loose brush. The trees bent and swayed.

In the park, he sat on a bench shadowed from the path lights by a low, wide palm. She sat beside him. She put her legs over his lap. She took his earlobe into her mouth. Without turning to look at her, he unbuttoned her jeans and slid his hand between her legs. For a moment, he was Lyle. He cupped his hand there, motionless, then removed it, refastening the button and wiping his finger on the paint-thick bench.

Egypt took her legs back, hugging her knees against her chest.

"I'm sorry," she said. "That was obviously a mistake."

"Yes," said Ropey. "Me, too."

They sat in silence, watching a group of speed walkers wearing medical masks do laps around the lake. Ropey opened one of his sardine cans and offered Egypt a fish. She took it. He took another, pressing it to the roof of his mouth until its bones dissolved. His cat was gone. He couldn't help but blame her.

"Okay," Ropey said. He stood. She stood. The air between them remained electric. Very aware of her crushable body next to his, he left for home. She followed.

Lyle stood in the middle of an empty lot. There had been a crumbling bungalow in this spot a few weeks before, but it had been recently bulldozed to make way for new development. The remaining foundation was shallower than Lyle would have expected. He knew nothing about Los Angeles. He'd grown up in a world of deep, carpeted basements with drop ceilings and paneled bars. Dried up leaves swirled around the bottom of the foundation. Lyle shook the treat bag. He called diligently for the cat.

Edendale

* * *

Megan watched Egypt and Ropey return to the house together from slightly farther up the road. Their body language made it obvious that they didn't see her standing there in the blustery hot dark. A hand on a shoulder. A mouth very close to a cheek. Two and two came together and the pit of Megan's stomach called out for Lyle. Of course Egypt would do this to him.

Megan stood in the wind until after they disappeared into the house, then followed them inside, where she filled the kettle with water and wiped the yard dust off the counter as she waited for it to boil. Once the rain had begun to fall, the areas that had burned would be subject to new danger. Without the roots of trees and brush to anchor all that loose California dirt, the hills would slide down toward the sea, taking roads and houses with them. Megan told herself that she empathized with the people whose houses had survived the fire only to be flattened by mud, but really, the prospect of the downpours washing away all the char and ash exhilarated her.

The kettle whistled. Megan poured three cups, green for herself and Ropey and chamomile for Egypt, leaving some hot water in the kettle for Lyle, who, bless him, was still out searching. She set out a mug for him and brought Ropey's tea into his room where he sat, still in his work shoes and clothes, on the edge of his bed.

"I made you some tea," she said, sitting down beside him. Ropey did not acknowledge her. "Maybe I'll just leave it here on the windowsill for you?"

Ropey shrugged, giving her a weak smile. Megan set the mug on the windowsill. She quivered with hatred and excitement. She left him and went up to Egypt and Lyle's room. Finding it empty, Megan went through the bathroom into her own room, where Egypt sat on the floor picking at her foot.

"Tea?" she asked. Egypt took it. Her eyes bugged over the mug like someone caught. Did she know Megan had seen them? It didn't seem possible, but still, the expression was there. Megan tried to formulate something to say, but this had nothing to do with her; this had everything to do with her.

The front door slammed open before she could decide.

"Guys?" called Lyle into the house.

"We're up here," Megan said. Egypt tensed beside her. Guilty, guilty.

Lyle came up the stairs and leaned on Megan's doorframe.

Edendale

"Are we calling it quits for the night?" His cheeks were flushed from the effort of his search. He wiped the sweat from his face, then pointed down to Egypt's foot. "Shit," he said. "What happened?"

Megan followed his gaze. The skin on Egypt's foot displayed a network of pink bubbles, white puss leaking out onto Megan's quilt.

Egypt pulled her foot underneath her. "Nothing," she said.

Simultaneously, their phones blared emergency alerts.

"There's a fire in Northeast," Megan said.

Lyle squinted at his phone. "We're not in the evacuation area. It's just a warning."

"What does that mean?" asked Megan.

"Just to be aware."

"That's it?"

"That's it."

"Well," said Megan. "What do we do now?"

"We go to bed." Lyle held out his hand for Egypt, who took it and followed him through the bathroom into their room.

5.

Megan slept fitfully, dreaming of fire, of rain, of Egypt's mouth on Ropey's skin. In the morning, she checked the internet from bed: last night's brush fire took two houses and part of a school. The forecasted rain had slipped further into the future. She found herself packing a go-bag. Jeans, clean tees, lots of underwear and socks. She zipped the duffel, embarrassed though alone.

"Hey," said Megan to Lyle on their way out to their respective cars. "I think you need to ask Egypt what's going on between her and Ropey."

She did not wait for his reaction. Instead, she unlocked her car and slunk in, throwing her duffel in the back and staring at the center of her steering wheel.

He knocked on her window. She rolled it down. Though the air smelled cleaner than it had the night before, the wind still blew hot and dry.

"You're not a part of our relationship," Lyle said. Megan's stomach clenched.

"What? I know that. Why are you telling me that?"

"I don't think you do, Megan. Egypt and I are going to get married and build our own life. You're a great friend, and that's great, but I'm going to be her husband."

But you and I are partners, Megan didn't say. We're the grownups, the parents, her keepers.

"Okay, yes I know," Megan did say. "I'm really happy for you. But, like, just ask. Something's weird." She rolled up her window and took ten deep breaths to center herself. As she drove to school, she listened to a public radio story about the connection between the wildfires and everything else wrong in the world: climate, housing, political rifts.

"We talk about climate change like it's a future threat," said the expert from DC. "But look at California. It's unlivable."

At school, there was nothing to do: Megan's bulletin boards were bright and relevant, her lessons and materials prepped for the next two weeks. But she was there, early. She wiped down the sink, opened the blinds, and straightened her desk. She opened the literacy drawer of her file cabinet, closed it, then opened it again. Rain, rain, come today.

"Shit." Megan lifted *The Big Book of Carnivores* out from between files. "Okay," she said to her empty classroom. "Okay."

She brought the book to her desk. *Dear Lucas*, she wrote in the first blank page. *Even grown-ups make mistakes! Please take* The Big Book of Carnivores *home forever. It is a gift from me to say, "I'm sorry!" You are an honest and trustworthy boy. It is such a joy to have you in my class! Love, Ms. Bell.*

Megan read the note over. She underlined "honest," and "trustworthy," blew the ink dry, and closed the cover with a satisfied pat.

6.

Ropey woke with the hot sun on his bed, dazed by the heat again.

The first thing he knew upon waking was that Captain America was lost. The second was that Megan and Lyle were at work and he couldn't stay in the house, not with only her.

He fled with a book and a beach towel to a different park, this one with no shade trees, only small, clipped bushes in beds of fragrant mulch. Beyond a chain link fence lay the reservoir, which the city had covered with gray plastic balls to prevent evaporation. He opened his book. The margins overflowed with notes made in pencil: Lyle. Ropey snapped the thing closed, put it behind his back, and looked out over the covered water. Mulch bits, picked up by the wind, whipped at the back of his neck. Still, until Megan got out of school, it would only be Egypt at home. He left the park and paced the neighborhood, seeking out the blocks with the most humans, glorious humans. He'd never understand people who claimed they felt alone in a crowd.

Near the middle school, he fell into step behind two boys. He stuck with them for a few blocks, feeling comforted by their book bags and baseball caps. He'd once been a boy with a book bag and a baseball cap, and so had Lyle. Separated by half the length of a continent, they hadn't known each other, but might as well have. Ropey thought of playground friendships cycled through. What the four of them were missing now was play. None of this was any fun! He could bring the mancala back out. Or he could go find a place to live with some chiller vibes. The world was filled with empty, shitty rooms and roommates willing to get high and grab burritos.

The boys stopped at a crosswalk and Ropey edged in front of them, realizing that he probably looked like he was following children, which he was, but not out of malice. The trees rattled. Ropey looked up, spotting only one not-so-promising cloud in the sky. November had broken its promise. Last night's fire had taken two homes and the wing of an elementary school before crews were able to contain it. This did not happen so deep into the city. Now, though the hot wind still whipped around the dirt and dried bits of sticks and leaves, there was an eerie stillness lying over Edendale. The cat was lost. He'd stuck his hand down Egypt's pants. Oh dude, he imagined himself saying to Lyle, if you're hurt about that, just wait until you hear what the two of us have done *emotionally*.

The walk signal lit and the two middle-school-aged boys stepped around Ropey into the street.

"If there were a school shooter," said one boy to the other, "which girls would you save?"

The speaker mimed a machine gun, throwing his body back as he sent off invisible rounds. The other boy pretended to wrestle it out of his grasp. Ropey followed the boys across the street, grabbing each by the arm as they stepped onto the opposite curb.

"What the hell," said the machine-gun boy, yanking his arm away. Ropey dropped the other boy's arm, surprised at himself.

"You shouldn't joke about stuff like that," Ropey crouched down to look the boys directly in their faces. "That's really serious stuff.'"

"Uh, okay dude. Thanks for the PSA."

The boys jogged away, nudging each other and glancing over their shoulders. After half a block, they turned, fired an invisible round into Ropey, and broke into a run.

Everyone deserved a million chances at peace and love, but Captain America was gone, and Ropey was beginning to wonder himself if the rain would ever come.

7.

Egypt woke alone. Damp sheet wadded around her legs; forehead, palms, feet pressed to the cool wall beside her. The nightstand clock read half past one. She dragged her tongue along the grime of her molars and strained up to tug the blackout curtains against the hot, autumn light.

Egypt rolled from her right side to her left. She flipped her pillow, finding its underside also very warm. Egypt, alone in the house, tried very hard to get the cat out of her head. She'd seen him around every corner last night as she'd wandered the house, failing to sleep. He'd slithered through doorways and under furniture. Ropey was out. She wanted him to come home. She felt they needed to talk.

She noticed that the blackout curtains didn't darken the room all the way. She closed her eyes.

It was past three when she woke again. Egypt threw the sheets off the bed. Her bladder ached. She walked into the bathroom. On the mirror above the sink, a yellow Post-it from Lyle:

Happy Tuesday, love of my life. I believe in you.

Egypt plucked the note from the mirror and held it against her mouth. She tiptoed into Megan's room and yanked her dresser open, choosing a clean pair of floral briefs, a pair of jeans, and a white tee shirt. After cinching the jeans around her waist with Megan's braided belt, Egypt sat on the bed, her weight loosening the tucked quilt, and rolled the denim to expose her toes, her feet, her ankles.

8.

"Lucas," said Megan from her desk during tidy-up time. "Once you've put those blocks away, I have something to show you."

Lucas set down the Rubbermaid of blocks directly below their cubby. Megan suppressed her annoyance with a kind smile as he walked to her desk, reminding herself that she'd wronged this little person. She took *The Big Book of Carnivores* from her bag and squatted down to his eye-level.

"I made a mistake." She explained that she was very sorry and that she'd like to make it up to him. As she spoke, Lucas looked only at the book, his focus so unwavering that Megan wasn't sure if he was listening until she told him the book was his, and he yanked it out of her hands. Lucas slipped the book into his backpack and joined the rest of the students in line for dismissal. Parents arrived and her classroom emptied. Alone, Megan turned off fluorescent overhead lights. The Rubbermaid of blocks waited on the rug. It seemed that everything in the world was up to Megan. Responsible people were punished for their competency instead of rewarded. As Megan knelt to lift the blocks into their cubby, Ms. Podeilski-Little appeared in her classroom doorway, holding six tomatoes up by the vine.

"I left a bowl in the faculty room, but I thought I'd bring you some, special."

"From your garden?" Megan asked.

"Yep. Straight to you."

Megan thought of taking them home, thought of home, thought of other places and other people. People who'd need her less. Where would she live if it weren't for Egypt? Somewhere the rain didn't disappear from the forecast?

"You're the sweetest," she said to Ms. Podeilski-Little.

9.

Driving home, Lyle passed an open house. On impulse, he pulled over and parked his car.

It was a small, white bungalow on a tree-lined street, flanked by two identical homes. The bungalow's front door was propped open, lanterns flickering in invitation on either side. Everything gleamed with a fresh coat of paint—the door, the narrow front porch, the twin rocking chairs that faced the street—and all the shrubs in the front garden were very small and very separate, islands of green in a vast sea of white gravel. This newness excited Lyle. He could see himself and Egypt on the front porch, also fresh and gleaming. They'd rock in synchrony. They'd twiddle each other's fingers in the gulf between their chairs.

Still, a line of tightness ran from his throat into his belly. Megan's comment had been constricting around him all day. At work, he'd felt constantly on the verge of either tears or vomit. Lyle considered himself patient, kind, a man capable of great feats of forgiveness. But Egypt had not yet asked.

He entered the house. Straight inside, the realtor stood at the kitchen island in conversation with a pregnant woman and a tall, bearded man. The tiny house seemed to be only kitchen, with one low, angular couch positioned by the front door in a failed attempt to signal "family room." The bearded man nodded at Lyle, putting his arm around the pregnant woman. Hello, other male, look what I have done. Lyle nodded back.

"Feel free to take a look around," the realtor called to Lyle, "I'll be with you in just a few."

Lyle wandered through the only door off the main room, discovering a bedroom. There were two doors inside. One opened to reveal a newly tiled bathroom, the other a walk-in closet set up like a nursery. Above the crib, a mobile of pastel ducks hung in the stagnant air. Lyle gave it a spin. He'd always imagined that Egypt would have difficult pregnancies. More than once, he'd had fantasies of her pale and swollen beneath hospital sheets, him having urgent hushed conversations with the doctor in the hall.

The realtor leaned against the doorframe.

"Full disclosure," she said, "I'd be surprised if those two didn't put in an offer tonight."

"It's a nice place."

"Up-and-coming neighborhood," said the realtor. Lyle thought of the freckle on the bone of Egypt's right wrist, and how she once blew her nose on the neck of his shirt and then fell over laughing.

"How late will you be here tonight?" he asked.

"Another forty-five," said the realtor.

He looked over his shoulder in the direction of home.

The realtor nodded. "My contact information is on the bottom of that sheet if you'd like to schedule a time to come back with your—"

Lyle neglected to fill in the blank.

"Let me show you the kitchen," the realtor said.

"Great," Lyle said, following her back out.

In the kitchen, Lyle knocked his fist on the counter. Solid stone. The cabinets were well made. Clean middle-grade appliances. Of course, he couldn't buy her a home in this city. He didn't even make enough to rent the two of them a studio apartment. Desire for another, simpler life flickered through him. A suburban subdivision in the Midwest, a long, low, carpeted home where she could mope around all day believing that the reason for her discontent was because she'd never made it to LA.

"She'll love it," he said. The assertion terrified him.

* * *

Edendale

At home, Lyle found Egypt in their bedroom. He took each of her hands in his and asked her straight out.

"Megan told me to ask you what's going on between you and Ropey. Why did she ask me to do that?"

"I don't know," said Egypt. "Why does anyone do anything they do? Our actions are all so random. It makes me feel alone, like I'm living in a world populated by bodies reacting instead of humans deciding. Do you know what I'm saying? Do you understand how I feel?"

"This isn't the kind of conversation I want to have."

"Well, it's the kind of conversation I want to have," said Egypt. Her face condensed to a sour point. "Ropey would have this conversation with me."

The couple sat in silence, each trying to listen to the other's mind. Instead, they heard Megan come home, then Ropey. Each roommate took a turn in the bathroom, then crept back down the creaking stairs into the kitchen where they spoke in low voices. Though neither Egypt nor Lyle could make out what their roommates said to each other, they did hear their own names and mention of the cat. Egypt put her hand on Lyle's shoulder. Lyle shrugged it away.

10.

And, in a thicket fifty yards up the hill from the house on Lemoyne, Captain America remained hidden, no longer whole. The edible flesh was torn from his body, exposing a mess of ligaments and bones. His hind right leg rested on a pile of leaves two body lengths back from its socket and, at the base of a honeysuckle bush, something red and walnut-shaped glistened. The muscle and jelly fat of the cat's soft underside were on the other side of the hill, divided between the still-hungry stomachs of a female coyote and her three cubs. But here, his intestine wound out from his hollowed body, its severed end suspended in a tangle of thorns. When the wind blew, the intestine swayed.

11.

Palms cold, tongue pressed to the roof of her mouth, Egypt decided that the best thing to do was to tell Lyle everything she'd been feeling about being a person.

"But don't you feel like we're missing some sort of great communion? Like, if our love was real love, all the layers would fall away and our souls would glow so bright that they'd fuse together?" She thought of the woman on the beach. Maybe she wasn't so wise. Maybe she'd just given up before she'd found it. "I'm not naïve, I know I'm incorrect. I was just expecting more. The logical part of me keeps reminding me that it's those expectations that are off. The other, louder part keeps telling me that the problem is you. I'm scared that what we have isn't actually love and I could fall in real love with someone else. Possibly Ropey. Though I'm not in love with him yet."

Lyle dropped her hands. He sat on the bed beside her and clutched his stomach.

"Have you had sex with him?" he asked.

The question infuriated Egypt. Here he was, thinking about sex as she was trying to tell him about her agony.

"Yes," she lied, wanting to bring him to equal fury. She watched the blow land, his face melting into an ugly drooping mask. Her whole body felt very fluttery. Lyle was crying. *No no no*, she thought, *don't cry, punch me. Fight me. Tell me that I'm wrong.*

Egypt went to their closet, nearly tripping over the dormant, now dust-covered air purifier, and dug out an old purse. *The only time Lyle ever cries is when someone plays the National Anthem*, Egypt had said at many parties, would say at many more parties, for years to come. This wasn't true per se, but it got a lot of laughs and Lyle never objected. Plus, it felt truer than the truth. She felt like she was with a man who only cried when he heard the National Anthem. But this was only when she thought about Lyle or when she talked about Lyle. Lyle in the abstraction. Because when she looked at him, at each pore in his skin, at each loving follicle of hair on his forearm, she beheld something completely different.

From the purse, Egypt took the money she'd been hiding, most of it stolen from Ropey.

"We've been fucking every day all over the house and he gave me this money so I could pay you back for the bed so that I didn't owe you anything anymore."

Lyle made a choking sound. She handed him the money and he took it without meeting her eyes so she lifted his chin and kissed him hard on the mouth. Now, she finally felt him enter the room. In response, she lifted her dress up over her head and pushed her bony chest into his face. He took her by the waist and laid her down on the bed. She thought about how, when she was on her back, her tiny breasts disappeared into her armpits but the pillow of fat on her lower belly stayed put, protruding upwards. Self-conscious, she tried to sit back up. He pushed her back down by the shoulders. Her head bumped the wall behind her. Her chest constricted in fear.

"That hurt me," Egypt said.

"Yeah?"

"Yes. Don't hurt me."

Lyle made a sound. Egypt couldn't decide if it was a sob or a laugh. Then he rolled off of her to the other side of the bed. Panicked that he would leave, Egypt yanked down his shorts and stuffed his soft penis into her mouth. He made the sound again. She ignored him, licking and sucking desperately. She clutched at his hips, feeling that, if she could make him hard, something would be final, fixed.

"I think you do love him," said Lyle.

Egypt rested the side of her face on his thigh. "I don't know if I believe in love."

"You love him."

"I love you."

"You said you don't believe in love."

"I said I don't know."

Lyle's grip on her shoulder tightened.

"You're hurting me again." Egypt watched his penis grow erect. As always, she felt a dull sense of victory. Then he flipped her over like a doll, spread her knees, and entered her much more quickly than he usually did. Egypt gasped in surprise.

"Hold on," she said. "Not yet."

He covered her mouth with his hand. When she tried to pull it off, he pinned her hands to the bed. She hadn't been ready and now his penis felt very hot, almost barbed, as he yanked in and out of her. He seemed to be hitting some new wall of raw nerves lined up deep inside her at the end of each thrust. She kicked, first with vigor, and then listlessly, listening to their headboard slam, listening to someone shouting, someone sobbing. She bit Lyle's hand and realized that the someone was herself, but then a second realization—

Edendale

of course it wasn't—washed over her. Because if she was the one making all that noise then Lyle was doing this against her will, having sex with her against her will, which sounded sort of like rape, and that couldn't be. Because he was Lyle and she was Egypt. She'd just put his penis in her mouth. Egypt remembered that she hadn't actually spoken to the woman on the beach. There was no advice to contradict besides her own. She closed her eyes. She commanded her body to unfurl, which slightly eased the pain.

12.

Downstairs, Megan focused very hard on slicing the tomatoes. They were such perfect tomatoes. She wiped her wet face with the heel of her hand.

"I'm going up there," Ropey said.

"Don't you dare," Megan said. "They need their privacy. They need space to work things out."

"This sounds—"

"We don't know," said Megan.

"We don't?" said Ropey, but he went back into his room.

One slice turned to mush on the cutting board. Someday, Megan knew, she would be a person who owned very good knives. She just had to be patient. She thought about how, after graduation, when she drove with Egypt from DC to LA and they stopped for a night at Lyle's parents' house, Lyle's mom had nervously served them a chicken and green bean casserole, apologizing for the quaintness of her cooking like they were something more refined than broke college girls, like she could see their future as women with good taste and expensive kitchen things. Megan spent the night in Lyle's childhood bed, staring up at the glow-in-the-dark stars on his ceiling, all swirling outward from a crescent moon with a slim, smiling face. Lyle's bed was stiff. He later told Megan that his father raised him to feel there was something immoral about soft mattresses, but that being with Egypt had taught him that there was no shame in indulgence. The ability to bear discomfort meant nothing more than the ability to bear discomfort.

13.

Ropey lay on his bed, staring up at the ceiling. Who was he to pass judgement? Different people needed different things at different times. Ropey simultaneously knew and didn't know that he was fooling himself. He wanted to trust Megan's judgment. He believed—deeply, deeply—that Lyle was a good guy. Also, if he went up there, then what? Ropey reached up behind his head and grabbed the mug off his windowsill. Last night's tea was cool with a hint of ash. He finished it anyways and then brought the mug into the kitchen, where he sat at the table and avoided looking up at the ceiling.

14.

Megan fanned the sliced tomatoes on a plate with the basil and mozzarella and made a quick balsamic reduction to drizzle on top. She placed the plate in the center of the table. Ropey did not eat. Lyle came down. He sat across from Ropey, picked up a leaf of basil and held it in front of his face, twisting it by the stem. The men sat silently, sneaking glances at one another until Egypt came down. Her face was scrubbed pink, and she smelled like soap, her eyes slightly puffy from the effort.

Lyle salted a slice of tomato. He offered it to Egypt. She shook her head. Lyle ate the slice himself.

Megan picked up the shaker after him and salted the entire plate.

"Does anyone need anything else?" she asked. When no one answered, she took the last seat at the table. Ropey looked at Egypt.

"Don't look at her like that," Lyle said.

"I'm not—"

"It's okay," said Egypt, without looking up.

"What's okay?" Lyle asked.

"I don't know."

"Are you talking to me or to him?" Lyle asked. The desperation in his voice made Megan wince. Egypt did not answer. Megan stood, took out a serving spoon and four small plates, set the plates at each of their places, and sat back down with her roommates. Each spooned a bit of the salad onto their plates. Megan looked at Egypt, tried to read her mind.

"Did you guys grow up eating pomegranates?" Megan said. She didn't know what her mouth was doing. She just needed to fill the air. "I feel like they became a thing in, like, the last few years."

"I had pomegranates," Egypt said.

"Oh," said Megan.

"I didn't," said Lyle.

"I did," said Ropey. "The neighbors had a tree in the yard."

"Well," said Megan, "Things are pretty different for different people in different parts of the country." She ate a slice of tomato. It came back up all over the table, along with everything she'd eaten all day. Megan realized that she was crying, that she had been crying for quite a while. She knelt down on the floor beside Egypt's chair.

Edendale

"I'm sorry," she said, burying her head into Egypt's lap to avoid looking at Lyle. She loved Lyle. He was her second-best friend. "God shit Jesus I'm so sorry. C'mon we need to go."

Lyle closed his eyes. Ropey stood, turned, and went into his room. Megan led Egypt upstairs, where she packed her a bag while Egypt sat on the floor, looking at her hands. As Megan was rooting around for Egypt's deodorant, their phones blared an emergency alert in harmony. Egypt picked hers up.

"High wind advisory," she said. "Fire conditions."

"Okay," said Megan. "Okay."

Egypt did not seem to own deodorant.

"Where's your deodorant?" Megan asked.

"Huh?"

Megan thought of her own, waiting in her go-bag still in her car.

"Okay," she said. "Let's go."

Megan led Egypt down the stairs. Lyle still sat at the kitchen table, looking at his hands. Megan's heart did a little dip. She wanted to clean up her vomit, see if he was all right. Instead, she looked away and led Egypt out the front door.

15.

Megan drove them to the beach because west seemed the appropriate direction to flee, used her phone to check the area for hotel rooms, then realized everything out by the coast was too expensive and drove them an hour and a half back inland, where she found a cheap room with two double beds. Inside, with the door bolted, Megan realized she should have taken Egypt to the police or the hospital first.

"Actually, I think we should go to the hospital," she said.

Egypt, who'd just lowered herself fully clothed onto the bed furthest from the door, looked up in exhaustion. "Now?"

"I think there might be a rule about the number of hours that can pass."

Egypt got under the sheets. "I'm very tired. Do you think I can sleep a little, first?"

"I don't know. I think you're supposed to go as soon as possible."

"I just want to sleep."

"I think we should go."

"I don't want to."

"I'm not going to make you do anything you're not comfortable with. But I think we need to go."

"Can we go tomorrow?"

"Yeah," said Megan, understanding that they would not go tomorrow (*please, Meggers*, Egypt would beg, *I can't, I can't, please just take me home*). Relief flooded in. "I think tomorrow would be okay."

16.

"Dude," said Ropey to Lyle, knocking on his half-open bedroom door. He hadn't been in Egypt and Lyle's room for a while, preferring lately to sneak to the bathroom through Megan's room where there was light and the air smelled fresh. Through the open door, he watched Lyle pull the comforter up, covering dark stains on the sheets.

It was his duty as an enlightened human to listen, to find love in hate, to talk it out.

Ropey entered the room. The men sat in silence, breathing at each other. Outside, the hot wind beat branches against the house. Lyle's shoulders shook.

"Do you want to talk?" asked Ropey. While he was here, he might as well be present.

"Fuck off," said Lyle.

"What?"

"Fuck off."

Edendale

"I want you to be able to talk to me." Ropey wished he'd cry. She's not your fiancée anymore, man, he thought at Lyle. Then, his throat tightening, he realized that she maybe, actually, probably was.

"Get out of my room," said Lyle.

"I'm here for you."

"Get out. Now."

17.

The wind shook the hotel windows in their frames. Megan checked her phone. She resisted the urge to text Lyle. She opened the weather app instead.

"Rain isn't happening until early tomorrow, now," she told Egypt.

"Oh," said Egypt, without turning over to face her.

Megan texted Ropey. *What's going on over there?*

"Hey, Meggers?" said Egypt.

"Yes?"

"Could we turn off the lights now?"

18.

On Lemoyne Street, powerlines swayed and dry fronds clattered onto roofs. Above an abandoned lot, the trunk of a dead eucalyptus split. The tree fell, clipping a transformer on its way down and sending a shower of sparks into the lot. Candle-sized flames began chewing away at the tangle of dead and dying vegetation. The small fires grew, converged.

The moon rose. Neighbor dogs barked alarm. In nearby homes, sleeping tenants with their windows sealed against the constant bad air failed to smell the smoke or hear the popping of the sparks. The fallen eucalyptus caught, sending a fast plume of flames up toward the sky. The wind blew these flames sideways into a wall of cypress bordering an adjacent yard. The cypress caught, then the grass beneath, then the garden trees and the wooden siding of the house.

The wind carried a cascade of embers down the hill. The roof of a backyard shed began to smoke. A swath of dried out bougainvillea crackled to life. In the yard behind the house on Lemoyne Street, an ember landed in the dead grass at the base of the lemon tree. The fire licked upwards, darkening the trunk of the tree with its smoke. The trunk caught, then the leaves. Inside, Ropey rolled onto his back, his sleep growing hot and labored. The hill sparkled with half a dozen separate blazes. Houses, trees, backyard sheds. Plumes of black smoke curled up into the sky.

The lemon tree crackled. The flames, whipped around by the wind, rose past the second story window. Lyle, still asleep, kicked off the blood-stained sheet. A branch fell flaming off the lemon tree and landed on the picnic table, which caught.

19.

Lyle woke to smoke and pounding on the front door. Fire. He looked first to Egypt's side of the bed. Wake her, get her out. But, with more pain than relief, where she was and why flashed back into his mind. He pushed the fact out; he couldn't bear it.

20.

Ropey woke to heat and Lyle's hands on his shoulders.

"Fire," said Lyle, shaking him. "Fire. Dude, fire. Get up."

Ropey's body took over. He was out of bed; he was in the front hall; he was being guided down the front stairs by a helmeted firefighter. He lifted his shirt to cover his nose and mouth. The back of his arms and neck tightened with heat.

"Anyone else in the house?" asked the firefighter. "Any pets?"

"No," said Lyle. "Just us."

The firefighter led the men down the hill and deposited them, corralled and blanketed, with a cluster of neighbors. The neighbors were in various states of nighttime dress and undress. Bathrobes, exercise clothes, oversized tees worn as nightgowns. A dark-haired woman in scrubs cried softly into her hands. A teenaged boy studied his bare legs.

Edendale

The fire chewed away at the hill in expanding patches. Crews stood on truck ladders spraying water down onto the burning homes as sagebrush crackled between lots. A single palm blazed, its charred fronds crumbling to the street below. Ropey watched the white arcs of water, very conscious of Lyle at his left arm. A dark plume of smoke rose from their backyard and flames licked up from the roofline.

"Did you grab your phone?" Lyle asked.

"What?" said Ropey, "No."

"I could have grabbed mine," said Lyle, "It was right there. It wouldn't have even taken any extra time." He knotted his hands through his hair.

A woman in a bathrobe tapped Lyle's shoulder. The roof of the house on Lemoyne Street caught.

"Do you need to make a call?" she asked, phone outstretched.

"Thank you," said Lyle, taking the phone. He dialed from memory and began to pace.

The flaming palm collapsed onto an already burning house.

"Hi," said Lyle. "It's me. This isn't my phone. Please call back. There's—please call back."

He handed the phone back to the woman. "Thank you," he said. "A girl might call."

Sirens, chainsaws, helicopters dropping clouds of retardant on fence and grass. The crews were making progress. One home, though blackened and collapsed, seemed to be nearly out.

Lyle vibrated with fear. Ropey leaned away.

The house on Lemoyne was now missing its roof. The south-facing wall had caved and the back wall was eaten away by flames. The front of the bungalow, however, remained intact. The front door swung. Their discarded shoes waited in a heap on the porch beside the mat.

21.

When Egypt half-woke in the middle of the night to her phone lightly buzzing on the far nightstand, she realized nothing but that she was in a large bed by herself with acres of empty mattress sprawling unused behind her curved, defensive back. She did not answer her phone. Instead, she unfurled herself, softening her jaw and unclenching her fists, and slithered her left arm and leg into the still taut other half of the bed. She was alone, and the sheets were so cool, and the room was so dark.

In two years, she'll be married to Lyle. Though they'll continue to finance their lives with his ever-rising agency income, the sharp edge of dependence will dull for Egypt. Any recollection of the panic in her legs and stomach, of how sometimes she couldn't even lay down beside him, will be long gone. She'll find intermittent work in commercials, land some small TV roles, and then have three baby boys, all in a row.

Lyle will spend time with the boys out in the yard every morning before he changes into his suit and leaves for work. The nanny will come from nine to seven.

She will lose touch with Megan, but not Ropey. She will dye her hair red, then black, then platinum blonde. She will total two cars, surprise Lyle with a German Shepherd puppy on his forty-fifth birthday, and, once, drive through the night to retrieve Milo, her youngest, after he texts her from his college dorm something short and vague about feeling sad.

But, on this night, in this motel room with Megan, Egypt's only concern was the curious amount of space available to her body and how to fill it. She flipped, she swam, she hooked her feet on one edge of the mattress and hung her hands off the other, a diagonal slash across it. She rolled horizontal, then upside down, then back with her head on the pillow again. The quilt was stiff, and the air-conditioning reeked of mildew, but the bed was hers alone and so she swelled and swelled, a loaf of bread rising over the lips of the pan. When her body was finally certain that there was no space for anything but itself in the bed, Egypt descended back down into dreamless sleep.

Acknowledgements

First, writing a book is an extraordinary privilege. Thank you, universe. Thank you, luck.

More specifically, thank you to Edendale's many brilliant, generous readers: Tess Gunty, Lindsey Skillen, Lynn Pane, Bruna Dantas Lobato, Crystal Powell, Francine Shahbaz, Clare Sestanovich, Kate Doyle, Anna Mebel, Wendy Chen, Alexandrine Ogundimu, and Eric Sweder, may no one ever ask you to read so many drafts of the same thing ever again. Classmates at New York University, thank you for your time and intelligence. My impossibly wonderful monthly workshop group, your feedback and support has been indispensable.

Thank you to all my writing teachers for your knowledge and encouragement. Neelanjana Banerjee, thank you for nurturing the very first seeds of this manuscript. Rick Moody, thank you for listening, questioning, and inspiring.

I worked many day (and night) jobs while writing Edendale. Thank you to the supervisors who got it, to the parents who encouraged this babysitter to write after bedtime, and to the babies who stayed asleep. Thank you, New York University, for supporting me during the middle drafts of this project.

Thank you, Jane, Virginia, Shirley, Toni, Joan, and Joy.

Amanda Manns and Olivia Batker Pritzker, thank you for creating Creature, for choosing this manuscript out of the slush, and for shepherding it to completion with such care and insight. You are the editors of an emerging writer's dreams.

Thank you to my mother, father, and sister, whose love and support is the most magical fuel.

Annie, cat of cats, thank you for the companionship and inspiration.

And, with bottomless gratitude, thank you Andrew for being down in the trenches with me for every step of this project. How has anyone ever written a book without you?

Jacquelyn Stolos grew up in Derry, New Hampshire. She studied English and French literature at Georgetown University, where she won the Annabelle Bonner Medal for short fiction. For her masters, Jacquelyn was awarded the Writers in the Public Schools Fellowship to study fiction in New York University's MFA program. She has attended the Community of Writers Novel Workshop, the Tin House Summer Writers Workshop, and the New York Summer Writers Institute. Her short fiction has appeared in *The Atticus Review*, *Conte Online*, *The Oddville Press*, and *Bodega Magazine*. Jacquelyn lives in Los Angeles with her husband and cat. *Edendale* is her first novel.

CREATURE PUBLISHING was founded on a passion for feminist discourse and horror's potential for social commentary and catharsis. Seeking to address the gender imbalance and lack of diversity traditionally found in the horror genre, Creature is a platform for stories which challenge the status quo. Our definition of feminist horror, broad and inclusive, expands the scope of what horror can be and who can make it.

Milton Keynes UK
Ingram Content Group UK Ltd.
UKHW012319230124
436569UK00005B/162

9 781951 971014